RETUNED - The Price of Time

Everhide Rockstar Romance Series – Book 6
by
Tania Joyce

EVERHIDE
ROCKSTAR ROMANCE

RETUNED – The Price of Time by Tania Joyce
Published by Gatwick Enterprises
First Edition: 2021 | Second Edition 2026
Brisbane, Australia.

RETUNED – The Price of Time : 2nd Edition
Everhide Rockstar Romance – Book 6
EPUB format: ISBN: 978-1-923653-12-2
Paperback: ISBN: 978-1-923653-13-9

Cover design by DesignRans and Gatwick Enterprises
Edited by CreatingInk

Tania Joyce: www.taniajoyce.com

To report a typographical error, please visit http://taniajoyce.com/contact-form
Visit www.taniajoyce.com to read more about her books and to buy books online. You will also find features, author interviews and news of her author events.

Keywords and subjects
Rockstar romance, new adult romance, contemporary romance, friends-to-lovers romance, accidental pregnancy romance, celebrity romance, music romance, band romance

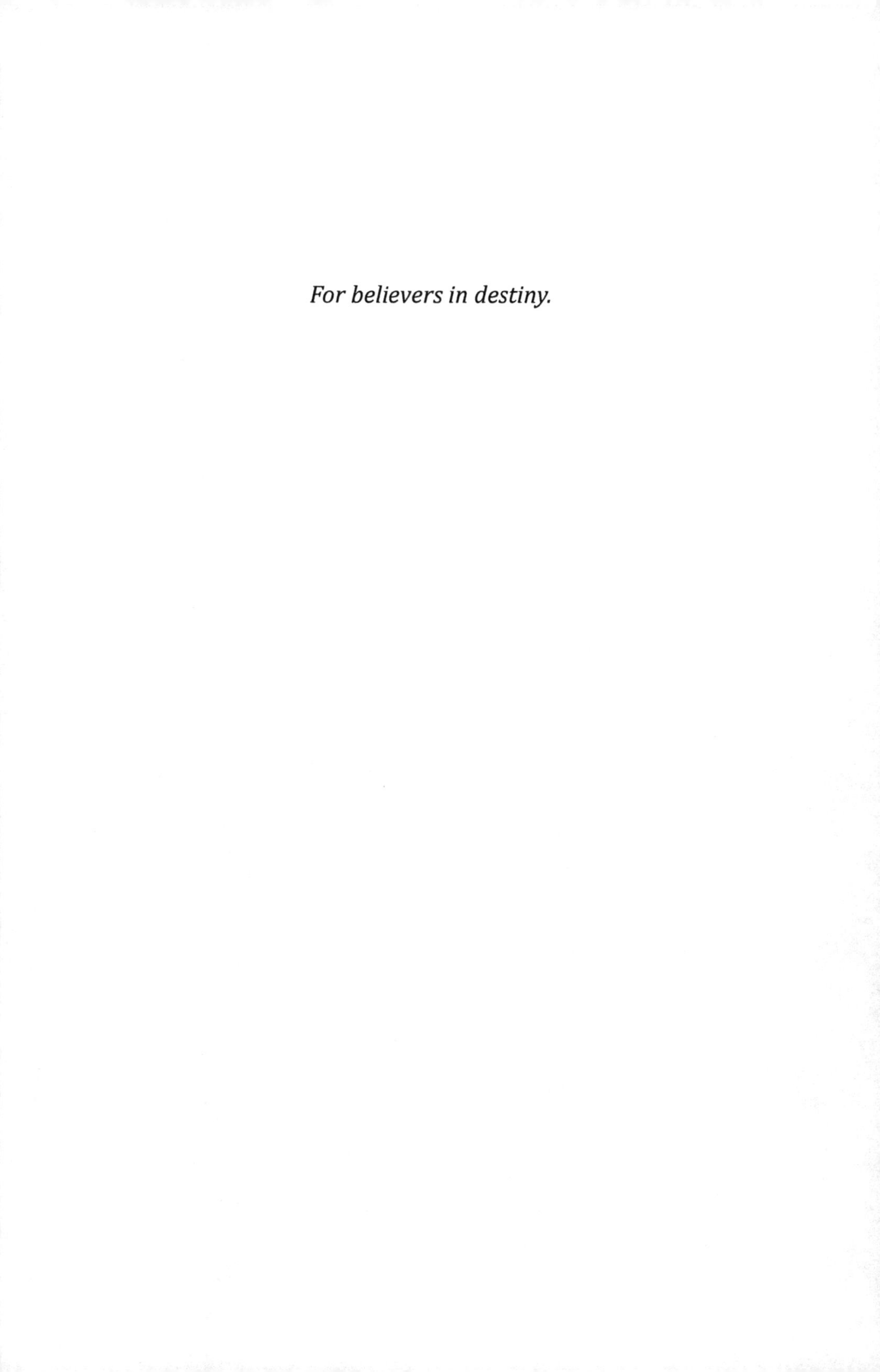

For believers in destiny.

Chapter 1

GEMMA

The cabin door slammed against the wall. I crushed my body against Kyle's, pressing him up against the wood. Sneaking in a six-day getaway before Christmas performances and appearances was just what we needed.

And I planned on making the most of every second.

"Damn, Gem." Dipping his head, Kyle seared my lips with a kiss. "Do you think we could've waited until we made it all the way inside? Until the heat kicks in?"

"No." I peeled his coat off his shoulders and tossed it on the floor inside the entrance. "It took too long to get here."

"At least we made it before the snowstorm."

Just. Wind howled and rattled the cabin's windows. Snowflakes swirled around the porch only to be swept away by the next unrelenting whoosh of air.

"That is a bonus." I tugged on his sweatshirt, drew him into the cabin and kicked the door shut. I ripped off my jacket, scarf, and gloves, and dropped them onto the floor by Kyle's coat.

Our flight from New York to Denver had been delayed by half an hour. The *supposed-to-only-take-ninety-minutes* drive from the airport to Breckenridge had taken us two hours. Finding the secluded cabin in the fading daylight had taken longer than expected. But it was worth it. The luxurious lodge that one of our LA-based friends owned was magnificent. High, smooth stone-featured walls gave way to massive windows that overlooked the valley below. Steepled wooden ceilings scaled above the open-plan living room and kitchen. Comfy beige sofas covered in cushions and throws surrounded the fireplace. And there wasn't a neighbor for miles, other than Sam and Chester, our security guards, who were staying in the guest cabin out back. They were under strict orders not to disturb Kyle and me tonight.

I reached for Kyle's belt and yanked open the buckle. "We have six days here. I plan to take full advantage of having you all to myself. You okay with that?"

His espresso eyes darkened. "Uh-huh." His calloused fingertips grazed against my cheeks, then his thumb glided across my lips. "I'm all yours."

"Good."

Placing my hands on his hard chest, I guided him toward the sofa. The moment his knees hit the edge, he sank onto the cushioned seat. The smoldering smile that curled the corner of his mouth heated my blood. After three years of marriage, our honeymoon phase hadn't ended.

I reached for the button on his jeans, popped it open, and unzipped the fly. Clutching onto the denim at his hips, I tugged them down. "It's still cold in here, but I promise to warm you up."

He chuckled and raised his hips so I could pull off his jeans and boxer briefs. "It won't take much if you keep going like this."

I yanked off his snow boots and clothes and tossed them aside. Standing before him, I toed off my UGG boots and slowly unbuttoned my jeans. My heart drummed with a wicked beat. My core begged for some action—but I was in the mood to play. Drawing in a deep breath, I wriggled and swayed my hips and took a step toward him. "You want me to tease you?" I lowered my voice, slipping in a touch of sexy seduction. "Strip slowly? Give you a lap dance?"

His scorching gaze raked over my body like he wanted to feast on me. *Yep.* He could have me for breakfast, lunch, and dinner. He shot forward and yanked my jeans and panties down to my feet. "Babe, you can do all those things . . . later. Just come here. Now." He caught my hand and tugged me forward.

Giggling, I kicked off my clothes and straddled his lap. Heat flushed my skin as our half-naked bodies connected. *Mmm.* Nothing better than some bare flesh on bare flesh. Kyle dragged the throw off the back of the sofa and draped it around us. The heating was slow to kick in.

Threading his fingers underneath my long brown hair, he caressed my head and drew my mouth toward his. "This is definitely better."

Just being close to him was heaven. It made my soul complete and my heart deliriously happy. I rocked my hips, slid my bare pussy against his hard cock and teased my opening against the tip. "Yeah? What about now?"

"Even better." He brushed the end of his nose against mine. His breath warmed my cheek. "We have no rehearsals for a few days." He nipped and sucked on my bottom lip. "No meetings. No shows. No Christmas chaos. This is perfect." As he kissed me, he flicked his tongue into my mouth. The taste of the dark chocolate we'd eaten during the drive tantalized my taste buds, rich and hot. And just like chocolate, I wanted more of him. More kisses. More closeness. More sexy wickedness.

I circled my hands over his broad, toned shoulders and squeezed his taut arm muscles. "All we're gonna do is snowboard . . . and this." I slipped my hand between us, curled my fingers around his cock and nudged it against my hot, wet arousal. *Tease. Tease. Tease.*

Oh, who was I kidding? I wasn't in the mood for delaying gratification.

Taking my weight onto my thighs, I mounted him, plunging his entire length deep inside me. Tingles shot up my spine and shivered across my skin. *So. Damn. Good.* When I was connected to Kyle, all in my world was right.

A hungry groan rumbled deep in his throat. His eyes fluttered shut. "Maybe we should skip the snowboarding. I'm down with just this." A sexy smile curled across his lips as he slid his hands underneath my long-sleeved sweatshirt and circled them up my bare back. "Hmm. No bra?"

"Nope. Too uncomfortable while traveling. And . . . not necessary." Having small boobs was a good thing; they never got in the way.

His eyes glinted golden. His hands were quick to work their way around to my front and cup my breasts. He massaged them and dragged his thumb across my nipples, sending them into hardened peaks. "One less item of clothing to get you out of."

Threading my fingers through his hair, I clutched at the short strands. "No time for more undressing." Our shirts and socks could stay on . . . for now. Digging my knees into the sofa, I drove my hips forward, taking his cock deeper. "Just let me fuck you."

"If you insist."

His kiss stole my breath. His warm, delicious lips and the hot swirls of his tongue fueled my pulse and charged my heart. The scent of his spicy cologne intoxicated me. Every time his hands brushed my skin, he fed my core with burning want, ravenous need, and hungry anticipation. Our bodies fit perfectly together. We were perfect soulmates. Perfect in love.

He caught hold of my hips. Digging his fingers into my flesh, he tugged me closer, thrust and penetrated deeper.

He hit just the right spot. With just the right pressure. With just the right friction.

"God, I love you," he whispered over our kisses.

"That's because we're made for each other."

"Yeah." His voice drifted. His thighs tensed. His grip tightened. "Gem?"

"Don't stop, babe." My breath panted in time with my racing heartbeat. "I'm there with you."

I rocked. He thrust. Deeper. Harder. Deeper. Harder.

Then, he stilled.

"Fuck." His hips jerked. His body shuddered. He filled me with his release as his cock throbbed and thrummed and pulsed.

My insides clenched around him. Like a lightning strike, my orgasm exploded. Electric waves spiraled through my body, zapping my nerve endings, scorching my blood, and blazing through every cell.

A lazy, bliss-filled grin lit his face. My heart flooded with warmth. Nothing beat the look of ecstasy on his face. And I was the lucky one to make him feel that way.

Panting to catch his breath, he nuzzled and nibbled on my earlobe, then kissed the hollow of my neck. "Damn, that was good."

"Always." I swept his dirty-blond hair off his forehead, his skin hot from the exertion. "Promise me we can do this every day while we're here."

"Promise," he said, rubbing his hands up and down my back. Then with a flick of his hand, he tapped my ass. "But before that snow gets worse, we'd better bring our gear in from the car and get a fire going."

While I'd be happy to stay here with him buried inside me, it was time to move. I eased off his lap, grabbed my panties off the floor, and slipped them on. I tossed Kyle his clothes and pulled on my jeans. "How about I make the fire while you grab the gear?"

He yanked on his boxer briefs, then his jeans. "You just want me to go outside and freeze my balls off, don't you?"

"I like your balls. So no." I pulled on my UGG boots. "I just know you'll do it because you love me."

"That I do."

After a quick kiss, we set to work. Within minutes, I had a fire taking hold in the hearth, and Kyle had made several trips to our rented Lexus four-wheel drive to bring in our food, bags, guitars, and snowboards. As I unpacked our groceries in the kitchen, Kyle came in with the last load of luggage and dropped it at the foot of the staircase.

"Looks like we'll get an awesome dump of snow tonight. Fresh powder to hit the trails tomorrow."

"That's fantastic." I pulled out a bottle of wine from our box of groceries. The snowfall had been stellar this season. All the resorts were open, and the mountains were ready to be carved up. "Shall we celebrate our little getaway?"

"Absolutely. Wine, you, by the fire? A perfect way to end the day."

I savored our escapes. Since we'd finished our world tour six months ago, we'd had a constant work schedule before it had turned crazy in the past month. Hunter, our fellow bandmate, had married my best friend, Kara, back in June, and had taken it easy to spend time with their daughter, Ashleigh.

But the break was over.

When we headed home to New York at the end of the week, we had to perform at a Christmas concert, and then after the New Year, it would be time to schedule our next album. We'd write new music after the awards season and plan the next tour.

My pulse skipped just thinking about it. I couldn't wait. For the first time in years, the road ahead was clear. Everyone was happy. In love. Focused. Ready. Nothing would stop us from making more hits and taking our music on the road. Absolutely nothing.

Chapter 2

GEMMA

"Oh shit. Shit-shit-shit-shit. SHIT!"

I ripped off the bed quilt, dashed over to my bag on the floor by the closet, and rummaged through it, tossing aside clothes and peering inside my toiletries bag. My head pounded like the wind against the cabin's bedroom window. *Crap.* This couldn't be happening.

"Babe? S'up?" Kyle rolled onto his side and tugged the pillow underneath his head. His bedroom eyes begged me to return to him and make love again, like we'd done last night and had repeated this morning.

But panic seized my throat. My pulse rang like sirens in my ears. I rummaged through my toiletry bag once more. "I left the fucking pill at home."

The blood drained from my face, leaving me dizzy. I could picture the packet lying next to my alarm clock on my nightstand. I hated that I'd had to have my contraceptive implant taken out. But my doctor had advised me to do so after I'd reacted to the new brand and had suffered from crippling cramps and heavy periods. The damn thing was supposed to prevent them, not make them worse. I just wasn't used to taking a pill every day.

"O-kay." Kyle's eyebrows pinched together. "Just call our

doctor after breakfast and have her email a prescription to the drugstore down in the village. We'll pick it up later today. I need to buy some Band-Aids, anyway. My snow boots always rub and give me blisters."

"You don't understand." I placed my hand over my stomach to stop the nausea from pooling. "This is serious. I could be pregnant."

"Gem, you're not likely to get pregnant after one day of missing the pill." Fear darkened his eyes. "Are you?"

"No." *Wait.* Did I take my pill yesterday morning? *Nope. Crap.* Otherwise, I would've packed them. In the rush to get ready to leave, it had completely slipped my mind. "But I've missed two."

His face blanched. "Oh, fuck."

Fuck, all right. "When we go out, I'll grab the morning-after pill, Plan B—or whatever-the-fuck it's called these days emergency contraceptive—to be on the safe side. I don't want a fucking baby." I stuffed my clothes back into my bag. "Ugh. I'm so angry at myself. I've been on birth control since I was seventeen. How could I forget? I'm so stupid."

Kyle propped his head on his palm and smoothed his other hand over the mattress, ironing out the wrinkles in the bedsheets. "Would it be so bad if you were pregnant?"

My eyes widened. "What the fuck?" I shrieked. "Yes, pregnant is bad. Real bad. I don't want kids. Not ever."

"Not even one day?"

The longing in his voice was new. It struck me hard in my chest. He couldn't want kids. He'd always been against them too. This wasn't happening. *No. No. No.*

"We're nearly thirty, Gem. Don't you want to consider it?"

Fuck. "No. I don't." I was up now; I may as well get dressed. I grabbed some panties and pulled them on, then yanked on some sweatpants, a shirt, and hoodie. I plonked down on the bed beside him. My knee rested against his hip. "You know me better than anyone. I don't have that need, that desire, or want inside me. There isn't a maternal bone in my body. I love our life, our family of friends, and our career just the way it is. I love us. Music and you are all I need."

"I know." He entwined our fingers and held them against his bare chest. "I'll love you until the end of time, no matter what. But I wouldn't say no if you changed your mind."

My vision blurred; my head throbbed. He'd married the wrong girl if he wanted to hear the pitter-patter of little feet. "You want kids?"

"Well . . . yeah. Maybe. If you do."

Shit. "Since when?"

He fidgeted with my wedding ring. "I guess since Hunt and Kar had Ashleigh. Seeing how happy they are is cool."

I lowered my chin. Hunter and Kara's happiness had come at a cost. They'd gone through the heartbreaking loss of their unborn child at twenty-four weeks and more devastating blows with two surrogate miscarriages. It'd be hard not to have concerns about having a baby. But I didn't want one. So it didn't matter. "They went through hell to have a child. I wouldn't have the strength to face what they'd endured."

"Yes, you would. We'd get through anything together." His brows pinched together. "Is the risk of losing a baby the issue?"

"No." My shoulders slumped. "I'm thrilled that Hunt and Kar finally had a baby. I love Ashleigh. But that doesn't mean I want children of my own. Kids are a life sentence. It's not something I want or need. I'm sorry."

"Don't be." He raised my hand and kissed it. "It seriously is okay. I just wanted you to know I'm open to the idea if you ever wanted to have a family. You are my life. Don't ever question that. I'm cool with not having kids too."

But his solemn gaze gave too much away. His tone held too much disappointment. There was no way I could contemplate having children. *Could I? Hell no!*

"Good. Because it's not going to happen." I nudged my knee against his hip. "Now, get up. We need to head into the village as soon as possible."

The sooner I got the pill, the better. I didn't want the stress and worry hanging over my head.

I tugged on my UGG boots and headed downstairs. But at the bottom step, I halted and stared out the huge windows. My heart faltered. Heavy snow fell. *Shit.* A thick blanket of white covered the road, the forest, and the Lexus parked on the driveway. Overnight, a foot of snow must have fallen, adding to the already present thick covering. "Ah . . . babe?" I called to Kyle. "I'm not sure we can go anywhere."

"Why?" He ambled down the stairs, tugging on his hoodie. "What's up?"

"We're snowed in." I pointed at the unrelenting dump. "Looks like it's set in for a while."

"Hmm. That's a shame." He stepped in behind me, wrapped his arms around my waist, and nuzzled into my neck. "I'm sure we'll find something to do to pass the time."

The wind picked up, rattling and hammering against the windows.

"But we need to get to town."

"We will. Once the storm clears." He spun me to face him and smoothed his hands over the back of my head. "I'll check in with Sam and Chester after breakfast. After that, if we still need to kill time . . ." He jutted his chin toward the staircase. "There's the spa in the master bathroom we could try out."

I jabbed my finger against his chest. "We can't have sex until I get the pill. Or condoms. Or something."

He caught my hand, wrapped it around his waist and tugged me closer. "We could do the ol' withdrawal method."

I giggled and shook my head. "I'm not risking it."

"Okay." He dipped his head and brushed his lips against mine. "Then there are a lot of other things we can do that are just as fun."

"I know. But—"

"Gem. Don't stress." He brushed his fingertip down the length of my nose. "You'll be fine. I promise."

I closed my eyes and prayed. *I hope so too.*

Despite calling my doctor after breakfast and the prescription being emailed through to me, I couldn't get to the village. The storm had caused severe damage. Fallen trees had blocked the pass down the mountain. There'd been a terrible accident on the road heading toward Denver. The blizzard had caused a whiteout. Sam and Chester couldn't even get from their cabin to the house. Everyone was snowed in. Even worse, the weather reports predicted more heavy snow for two more days.

Fuck!

By noon, the storm hadn't eased. By evening, another foot of snow had fallen. The following morning offered no reprieve.

We were stuck. For another day. No snowboarding. No pill.

I paced the length of the living room in front of the glowing fireplace. Kyle sat on the sofa, drinking a steaming cup of coffee. I flipped my cell phone around in my hands, praying for a solution. "Can we call someone? The local snowplow operator? Someone with a snowmobile?"

"Gem. Stop. No one can get to us in this weather." Kyle placed his cup on the coffee table. He stood, headed over to me, and wrapped his arms around me.

My cheek pressed against the soft fabric of his sweatshirt. He smelled of cinnamon and spice. His warmth enveloped me like a blanket, but his heartbeat raced too fast. He was worried too.

He kissed the top of my head. "Why don't we watch another movie?"

I grabbed a handful of his shirt and gave it a tug. I hated not making things happen at the click of my fingers like I could do in the city. Out here in the mountains, I had no personal assistant to work her magic—Bec was off seeing family for an extended Christmas break. No shops at my doorstep—the closest village was thirty minutes away. No home delivery—not in the middle of a snowstorm, anyway.

"Okay." I nodded. "I need something to distract me."

Curled up on the huge sofa next to Kyle, I settled into watching *Bad Boys for Life*. But I couldn't sit still. Couldn't concentrate. My mind ticked like a time bomb, calculating how long I had left until the emergency contraceptive pill wouldn't work. It had to be taken within five days of unprotected sex. *Shit.* I was in trouble.

I placed my hand on my rolling stomach. Was that nausea or stress? *Oh God.* Or a baby? What if I was pregnant? *Fuck.*

I'd always been diligent with contraception ever since high school. Implants and condoms had been essential during my wild and adventurous past. But now? How could I have been so careless with my husband?

There was no way I could have a baby. No way I'd ever want one. I knew who I was. Nothing would ever change my mind.

I closed my eyes and took a deep breath. I needed to get to the village. I needed that pill.

I hoped it wasn't too late.

Chapter 3

KYLE

"Gem. Stop." I caught her arms to stop her from climbing over the drugstore counter and decking the pharmacist. *Damn.* She could be feisty.

"No. I won't." Gemma's voice sliced through her teeth as she glared at the pharmacist. "Just give me the damn pill."

I didn't know whether to laugh or drag her outside and shake some sense into her. She'd done her best to keep her cool for the past five minutes, but she'd reached her limit. No matter how much we'd tried to draw on the pharmacist's sympathy and compassion, he wouldn't relent. While Gemma lashed out, my worry deadened my bones. This wasn't the outcome we'd expected.

"I'm sorry, Gemma. Miss Lonsd—I mean, McIntyre." The pharmacist's tone remained calm and adamant, but since he was dressed in a navy reindeer sweater and Santa hat decorated in tinsel and flashing lights, it was hard to take him seriously. "It potentially has been more than five days since you had unprotected intercourse. Therefore, Plan B won't work. I advise you to go to your doctor, have a proper pregnancy test, and take matters from there."

"Please." She placed her hands on the counter and pleaded. "I need that pill. I'm willing to pay you anything for it."

"It's not about money, Mrs. McIntyre," Alistair, the pharmacist, said. "The pill's effectiveness will be void."

Fuck. I rubbed my scruffy chin. After being trapped on the mountain for three days, we'd finally made it down to the village with our bodyguards in tow, only to be confronted by Mr. Do-What's-Right at the drugstore.

But this changed everything.

Concern had simmered in the back of my brain since Gemma had told me she'd forgotten the pill. Now, we had no quick fix. She could *really* be pregnant.

The fear in her eyes, the anger, the determination stabbed my heart. She didn't want kids. But that didn't stop *my* want from flaring. Having a baby would send our world into shambles. I didn't know how we'd make it work when we performed side by side, but I'd love a family. I placed my hand on the small of Gemma's back. I needed to hold on to her to stop my brain from racing off on wild tangents. I calmly spoke to Alistair. "Is there anything she can do?"

"Yes." Alistair gave Gemma a thin smile.

Her lip twitched like she wanted to punch him.

The pharmacist ignored her. "In a few days, you can take a home pregnancy test. The best results are at the ten-to-twelve-day mark after intercourse. Then you'll know if you are pregnant or not." He turned to the shelf behind him and grabbed a pink box. "This is the most common one we provide."

Gemma's cheeks burned red. "I don't want a fu—"

"Gem? It's okay." I eased in front of her and turned to Alistair. "Thank you. We'll take it." I grabbed my cell phone from my coat and paid for the package.

After Alistair placed the box in a brown paper bag, Gemma snatched it out of my hands. "Yeah. Thanks for nothing." She turned on her heels and stormed out of the drugstore.

I caught her arm outside the shop and pulled her to a halt. "Hey."

"What?" She glanced up at me. Worry etched her brow.

"You okay?"

"No."

That was obvious. "We can't do anything until we're back home. We'll do the test. Go to the doctor if needed." The notion hurt my skull. New emotions stirred in my chest. If Gemma was pregnant, I wasn't sure I'd want to get rid of it. Would this cause a rift between us? *Fuck.*

Gemma stared at the ground and nodded. "Okay. I just hate . . . waiting." She clenched and unclenched her hands. "I just want this over with."

"Me too." *Maybe . . . not.*

She lifted her chin, sucked in a deep breath, and pasted on a smile as fake as Dolly Parton's boobs. "Let's go boarding. At least we get one day on the slopes before heading home."

We'd gotten cabin fever. Being snowbound for days had been fun up to a point. Playing guitars and hanging out with Gemma had been awesome. Watching movies, reading, and enjoying each other's bodies in creative ways had been entertaining. But now we needed fresh air, the wind on our faces, and adrenaline coursing through our veins as we carved up the slopes. I needed to keep occupied so I wouldn't think about the pending test results.

I tightened her scarf and straightened her beanie. "Are you prepared for me to beat you down every run?"

"No chance." Fire ignited in her eyes. "I'm faster. Challenge accepted."

"Bring it."

We raced to our car and headed toward the slopes.

***

Back in New York, the morning after performing a set at the Christmas benefit concert at the Barclays Center in Brooklyn, I sat on the bed next to Gemma and stared at the countertop in our ensuite. The little white stick resting on top of the pink packaging seemed to glare at me, mocking me. My heart flipped and flopped. I'd been telling myself for days I'd be okay with either result, but in truth . . . I wasn't.

My gut curdled and crawled. If Gemma was pregnant, was there any way I'd convince her to have a baby? It crushed my heart knowing it would be a lost cause. What else could I do other than respect her decision? It was her body.

I flipped my cell phone around in my hands. The timer I'd set for the test counted down. Down. Down.

Minute by minute.

Second by second.

Gemma fidgeted with her rings. She was as anxious as I was.

The alarm went off. I swiped the screen to stop it.

This was it.

I turned my head toward her. "You ready?"

"Yes." Gemma stood and smoothed her hand over her stomach. "Let's get this over with."

She strode toward the bathroom door but stopped at the entrance. She sucked in a deep breath, let it out slowly, then stepped toward the counter. I held my breath as she picked up the stick and stared at it.

Her shoulders slumped. Tears welled in her eyes as she shook her head. "Fuck." She tossed the stick into the sink, dashed to the toilet, and threw up.

"Gem?" I rushed in and squatted behind her to rub her back.

She pounded her fist against the seat. "I didn't want this. I'm sorry. I fucked up."

I swept her hair into a ponytail and held it off her face. "It's positive, isn't it?"

She flushed the toilet. She tore off several pieces of toilet paper and wiped the tears from her eyes and her mouth. "Yep. Motherfucker."

Oh wow. Pregnant! Fevered elation shot through my veins like lightning, but it disappeared within a heartbeat. The backs of my eyes stung. I knew what this meant. I sank onto my knees and kissed the tip of her shoulder. Closing my eyes, I fought down the pain pummeling my chest. "It's okay." My voice caught in my throat. "We'll . . . deal with it."

She slid onto the floor beside him and leaned against the wall. "I know. I just didn't want to have to go through this." She thudded her head against the tiles. "It's annoying. I'm pissed. This shouldn't have happened. It's so screwed up."

"No. It was an accident." I took her hands and kissed them. "We'll get through this together. Always. But . . ." I had to let her know how I felt. What was in my heart. What *I* wanted. "Are you sure, Gem? Can we talk about this just for a sec?"

"There's nothing to talk about." She staggered to her feet and headed over to the basin to rinse her mouth. "I don't want kids."

I clambered upright and handed her the hand towel. "But I do. Does that change anything?"

"No." She wiped her face, then tossed the towel on the counter. She went to step around me, but I blocked her path.

We always talked things through. She had to hear me out.

"Gem. I lost my family." My parents had been killed in a car accident. I'd lost my sister to leukemia. Nothing, not even her love and Hunter's friendship, had ever completely healed that void. "My dad was a complete ass, but I loved my mom and sister. I remember vacations, and dinner conversations, and my mom teaching music. She inspired me to follow my dreams. We'd be like her with our kids." I cupped Gemma's face and pressed my forehead against hers. "Gem, I love you. You are my family. My life. My everything. I'm ready. I'd love to have a baby with you."

"No." She slapped my hands away and stormed into the bedroom.

I followed her. "Is it because you're afraid or because of what you went through as a kid?"

"Ah . . . both." She glared at me like I suddenly didn't know her. "My dad leaving and my mom never caring messed me up big time. My childhood was shit. But you know that."

She hadn't spoken to her gold-digging, backstabbing, sell-my-daughter-for-money mother in two years. Her life was better for it. I couldn't deny that.

"Gem." I clutched her upper arms. "You're nothing like your mom. You love and care for everyone around you. You don't have a cruel bone or intention in your body. You'd be a great mom."

She winced. Was the thought of motherhood so horrifying? But I knew what frightened her most.

"Babe, I'm not like your dad." Her father walking out on her when she was twelve had broken her heart. Him dying a few years ago and sending her a letter that implied he'd never loved her either had crushed her soul. "I'll never leave you. I love you too much. You're stuck with me forever."

She lowered her chin and shook her head. "I just don't want to be a mom." She took my hands in hers, then held them between us. "I never knew what family was until you and Hunt came into my life. You have given me so much love and support, it blows my mind. But this is more than turning out like my parents." She drew her shoulders back, and defiance set in her tone. "I know who I am. I know how I feel and what I want. A child wouldn't fit in with our lifestyle. We work insane hours. We're constantly writing, recording, away on promo and touring. A kid would screw up everything we've worked so hard for. I'm not going to throw away my career—neither are you. We love music too much."

"We'd never give up music." I squeezed her hands and gave them a gentle shake. "Not ever. We'd make it work. Hunt is. We'd hire help."

She pulled back. "Kyle. No."

The anguish in her voice tore my heart in two. I'd never want her to do anything she didn't want to. I splayed my hand across my heart. "I don't want us to get to thirty-five, forty, or forty-five years old and regret not having kids."

A flash of doubt flickered in her emerald eyes, but within a blink, it was gone. "We won't. We live an amazing, full life. Our legacy will be *our* love for each other and our music. Not children."

I closed the gap between us and caressed her face. She tilted her head back to meet my gaze. "Gem, you said you'd never love anyone after Ben all those years ago, and you did. You swore you'd never fall for Hunt or me, and you did. You were adamant that you would never marry, and you did. You've changed. I've changed. Having a baby would be an incredible step in our life together."

Steel set her jaw. "No."

I sucked in a slow breath to ease the ache in my heart. I'd always admired her strength, her courage, her confidence. For the first time in forever, we weren't on the same page. It hurt like hell. It had been nice to contemplate a baby, even if it was just for a moment. It just wasn't meant to be. "Gem." I swallowed the dry lump in my throat. "It's all right. I understand. I'd be okay if you weren't pregnant. But you are. You're carrying *our* baby. If there was a chance, any hint of a possibility that you wanted to have a child, I'd be down with it."

She shook her head and swayed on her feet. "There's no hint. I'm sorry." She dashed over to her nightstand and grabbed her cell phone. "I need to call our doctor. I need to take care of this as soon as possible."

This? . . . Our baby? I wiped my hand across my face and headed back into the bathroom. As she paced the bedroom, searching her cell phone, I clutched the edge of the countertop and stared at the pregnancy test lying in the sink. Two blue stripes filled the panel. *Positive. Pregnant. A baby.* My vision blurred.

Fuck.

A shudder ran down my spine. Gemma's gaze burned into my back. *Shit.* Telling her how I felt had made no impact on her decision. I had to smother the idea of having a child and set steel in my heart. I needed to be strong for Gemma. Support her. Be all she needed.

"Kyle?" Her voice was barely audible.

I sucked in a deep breath, wiped my wet eyes, and then tossed the stick in the trash. "Yeah. Coming."

As I wrapped my arms around her, she slid her hands around my waist. She pressed her cheek against my chest. "It'll be okay. Let's just deal with this so we can get on with life. It was my mistake. I'll fix it."

She rose on her tippy toes and kissed my lips, then turned away to call the doctor. After a minute of conversation, Gemma hung up and tossed her phone onto the bed.

"Shit." She sank onto the mattress.

"What is it?" I sat beside her and placed my hand on her back.

"The doctor is away until January sixth. I can't do anything until then."

"That's only two weeks away."

"I know. I just didn't want to have to wait that long."

"You'll be fine. Other than the throwing up." I pointed toward the toilet. "Have you got morning sickness?"

"Ugh. I hope not." She groaned as she rubbed her stomach. "I don't want to think about it anymore. Let's go downstairs and finish wrapping the Christmas presents. I want to keep as busy as possible for the next two weeks, deal with this issue, then move on."

"Gem? It's a baby. And it's okay to think about. If you want to cry, scream, curse, contemplate it or not . . . I'm here for you."

She rested her head against my shoulder. "Thank you. But I'll be fine. I promise."

I smoothed my hand over her head and toyed with the long strands of her soft, silky hair. "Do you want to tell everyone about this at Christmas dinner tomorrow night?"

Our close circle of friends had an uncanny way of finding things out. There'd be no way I could keep this from Hunter; and I wouldn't want to. If I told Hunter, then Hunter would tell Kara, then she'd tell Lexi, who'd tell Hayden.

Her shoulders slumped. "Guess they'll find out, eventually. I just don't want them to get in my face about it."

"They won't. They love you too much."

I wound my arms around her shoulders and pulled her close, holding her tighter than normal. I inhaled the sweet floral scent of her hair deep into my lungs. The pregnancy result still rattled my brain. *Gemma was pregnant.*

I lived for Gemma. Always would. It dented my heart that she didn't want kids. I wouldn't hesitate if she changed her mind. But the timing wasn't right. It never would be. I had to accept that. I loved her more than life itself; this was no deal breaker. I'd always respect her decision. I'd support her and stand by her side until the day I died. We just weren't meant to have a baby. But fuck . . . It'd be awesome if we did.

Nope. I wouldn't dwell on this matter. It was Gemma's choice.

Now I just wanted to put this incident behind us so we could get on with life.

That doctor's appointment couldn't come soon enough.

Chapter 4

HAYDEN

Holding baby Ashleigh in my arms, I rocked from side to side. I sang softly to her as I rubbed her little hand. Her big blue eyes stared up at me. Her tiny pink lips curled into a smile. I'd never been into kids until Hunter and Kara had Ashleigh. They were smitten with her. So was I. While Kara was busy preparing Christmas dinner, I took the rare opportunity to steal a cuddle. A ripple fluttered through the center of my chest. Yeah . . . I could do this. I'd like to have a family of my own.

Was Lexi ready to go down that path?

With her marketing, photography, and creative production career with Everhide getting busier, and with me about to work on new music with the band, would it be crazy to bring up having kids with her? The worst-case scenario was she'd say no. But was I prepared to head down this road if she said yes? *Absolutely.*

As I stood by the monstrosity of a Christmas tree that was covered in twinkling lights and baubles in the corner of Hunter and Kara's penthouse living room, I glanced at my friends in the kitchen. Kyle carved the meat for our Christmas dinner. Gemma stirred something in a saucepan on the cooktop. My stomach grumbled; I hoped it was gravy. Kara decorated a cake, and Hunter dashed around grabbing bottles of wine and glasses for the table.

The smell of roast turkey and chestnuts wafted across the room. As carols played softly through the sound system, my friends' laughter and clatter filled the air.

I drew in a deep breath. How fortunate was I to be spending another magical Christmas with them? My family. And the love of my life, Lexi.

With her blonde curls bouncing loose around her shoulders, she headed toward me. She shook a baby bottle in her hand, ready to feed Ashleigh. Her soft smile was as warm as the flickering gas fireplace embedded in the wall.

"Hey." She gave me a quick kiss on the cheek. "What are you smiling at?"

"You."

"Awwwwh!" She touched my cheek. "You're so sweet."

Then she kissed my lips. *Hell yeah.*

"Lex?" Kara called from the kitchen, licking frosting from her fingertips. "Don't forget to burp Ashleigh, please? Otherwise, she'll throw up."

"Will do." Lexi waved at Kara over her shoulder.

"There's a towel on the coffee table." Kara waved her frosting-covered knife at us.

"Got it."

I chuckled. Kara thrived as a mom. At first, she'd been overly possessive and protective of her daughter. After the hell she and Hunter had gone through to have a child, I understood totally. But she'd relaxed in her ways over the past couple of months. Thank goodness.

"Here, Angel. You can feed her." I slipped Ashleigh into her arms and straightened the baby's beanie and blanket.

"Thank you." Lexi's voice was barely above a whisper. She placed soft kisses on Ashleigh's forehead and sat on the sofa, bottle in hand.

I fell beside her. I hooked Lexi's curls behind her ear and kissed the side of her head. "You look very content with her in your arms."

Lexi gazed at Ashleigh gulping down her bottle. "She's just so beautiful."

Ashleigh was one gorgeous baby. Eyes as azure as Hunter's. Wisps of soft brown curls covered her head. A cheeky smile that stole your heart. With her gene pool, she was destined to be a stunner.

What would our kids be like? What did the future hold for me and Lexi? My stomach bubbled like beer. After a crazy couple of years, landing careers of our dreams, falling in love, getting married, and putting our parents' problems behind us, having our own family seemed like the next logical step in our relationship.

I hooked my arm behind Lexi's head and combed my fingers through her silky curls. "What would you say to having one of our own?"

Her head shot up. Her eyes widened. Her mouth gaped. "What? A baby?"

I shrugged my shoulder, just a fraction. "Yeah."

"But . . . but we haven't been married long. What about the new album? And the next tour?"

I buried my fingers in her curls and massaged her head. "Lex, we're nearly twenty-nine. We've been married for almost three years. With Hunt and Kar having Ashleigh, we can ensure that having kids on tour will be accommodated for."

She blinked and shook her head. "You . . . you want a baby?"

Had the suggestion muddled her brain? I hadn't meant to shock her. But seeing I was on a roll, I may as well dump all my thoughts about a family onto her.

"Yeah." I chuckled. "And if we do . . . maybe we should look for somewhere new to live. Somewhere near these guys, so we're closer to them for work." We spent a fortune on Uber fares and car parking fees. It would be ideal to be within walking distance of Hunter and Kara's home, or Kyle and Gemma's place, which was just down the laneway. But Tribeca was expensive. I wasn't sure we could even afford our own condo.

"But I love our place." Lexi's voice shook. "I don't want to move.

We've lived there for nearly ten years. It's our home."

For me, home was with Lexi. After being in and out of foster homes as a kid, I'd learned not to get attached to the four walls around me. But now, I'd changed. I wanted a place to call my own. Somewhere where we could raise a family and create new memories.

Convincing Lexi to move would be a challenge. She held on to things so tightly. Since her parents' bitter divorce, she'd craved stability. I wanted to give her that and more in our own home. "But . . . if we want a family, we might have to find something bigger." We barely fit in our tiny two-bedroom apartment. My drums took up a lot of space. So did Lexi's camera equipment.

She rounded her shoulders and pursed her lips. She glanced at Ashleigh, then at me. Her dark blue eyes shimmered silver in the soft light. "Oh my God. I . . . I—"

"Hey. It's okay." I kissed the tip of her shoulder. "It's up to you. Whenever you're ready."

She leaned toward me and kissed my lips. She tasted sweet, spicy, and all eggnog-y. Ashleigh ignored us, content, sucking on her bottle. Lexi searched my face, as if questioning whether I was serious.

Yep. I am.

She grazed her teeth across her lower lip and bobbed her head. "I . . . I . . . I'm ready too. You wanna do this? Have a baby for real?"

My heart soared. Clouds parted. Rays of sunshine filled my chest. "Yes. I do."

"Holy shit." Tears welled in her eyes. Ashleigh had finished her bottle, so Lexi placed the baby over her shoulder and patted Ashleigh's back. "You wanna start trying?"

I draped my arm across her waist and kissed her cheek. "That bit, I'm totally looking forward to."

Her cheeks turned rosy pink. "Me too. So as of now, no more birth control?"

Fear and excitement shimmered in her eyes; it charged and

skipped through my veins. I couldn't contain my grin. I wouldn't screw up my family like my drug-addict parents had done to me. I nuzzled against her ear, blew my warm breath onto her neck, and kissed beneath her lobe. "None."

She flinched and giggled. "You want to practice as soon as we get home?"

"Always."

Her eyes sparkled. Her chest swelled. "Okay."

I caught her chin with my fingertips, then brushed my lips against her sweet mouth. "I love you. So much."

"Yeah. Me too."

"Dinner's ready," Kyle called from the kitchen. He picked up his platter of carved turkey and headed toward the table.

Dragging myself away from Lexi, I slapped my palms against my thighs. "Good. I'm starving." I'd snuck in a couple of hours' practice this afternoon. Drumming always worked up my appetite. "And I'll need more energy for later."

I jumped to my feet and helped Lexi to stand. I kissed my blushing wife on the lips, then kissed Ashleigh on the head. The prospect of having our own little bundle of joy soon was the best Christmas present ever. I was sure my grin was as wide as the Mississippi River.

While Lexi placed Ashleigh in her rocker beside Kara's dining chair, I stepped up to the table. The entire surface was covered in red Christmas candles and green sprigs of holly, white dinner plates, silverware, wine glasses, and drinks, along with dishes of roasted meats, green vegetables, and mashed potatoes. The incredible aroma drifting from the food made my head spin and my mouth water.

"How's Ashleigh?" Kara pulled off her apron and took her seat at the head of the table. "She drink all her bottle?"

"Like a champion." Lexi placed the empty bottle in the sink, then sat on the chair beside me.

"What's the bet she cries halfway through dinner?" Hunter pinched his lips together and waggled his finger at his daughter, who was chewing on a teething ring. "Not tonight, hey? Give Daddy some peace."

I chuckled as Hunter took the seat at the other end of the table. Hunter gushed over his daughter. It was so cool to see my badass friend turn to mush over his child.

Opposite Lexi, Gemma pulled back her chair and sat down. "Can we just enjoy dinner without baby talk?" She poured a glass of water and took a big swig.

"Gem? Are you okay?" Lexi asked as she opened a bottle of red wine. "You don't look the best."

"I haven't felt well since yesterday." Gemma swiped her fingers across her brow. "But I'll be *fine* soon enough."

Maybe it was the way she emphasized her words, but something in her tone was off. I'd known Gemma for years and had grown closer to her during the tour. I'd gotten to know her quirks and mannerisms. Something wasn't right.

Her face lacked color. Her eyes held no sparkle. Her energy level hovered near zero. The tension in her jaw didn't ease.

"Gem?" I threw her a concerned look.

But before she could respond, Hunter raised his glass of wine. "First, a toast. Here's to another incredible year. To my amazing wife. My gorgeous daughter. To our incredible friendship. May we rock on, continue to make phenomenal music, and keep living life to the fullest."

"Abso-fucking-lutely." I hollered and raised my drink.

Everyone clinked glasses and sipped their wine. Except Gemma—she had more water.

"Dig in," Kara cheered and clapped, then waved at the food before us. "Thank you, Kyle, for cooking. I'll learn how to master a kitchen one day. I promise."

"You helped." He flicked a finger at the turkey. "Eat before it gets cold."

Everyone grabbed serving spoons or tongs and loaded their plates with food, but I couldn't dislodge the niggle between my shoulder blades that something more serious was off with Gemma.

And Kyle. I stabbed and cut a piece of turkey, then stuffed the meat into my mouth. Gemma pushed peas around her plate. Kyle played with his mashed potatoes.

Hunter seemed to sense their unease too, throwing them continual worry-filled glances. He ate a slice of carrot and then jabbed his fork in their direction. "Guys? What the fuck is up? You've been out of sorts for days. It's more than being tired after skiing and the concert, and the other crap you've been spinning my way for days. So spill."

The one thing I loved about this circle of friends was their brutal openness and honesty. No secrets. No lies. No bullshit.

"Fuck," Gemma mumbled, staring at her plate.

Kyle placed his cutlery down, turned to her, and rubbed her back. He leaned toward her, kissed the side of her head, then rested his forehead against her hair.

She lowered her chin and furrowed her brow. Then she sighed and flicked her hand at him.

I loved how these two didn't need words to communicate. A touch, a glance, a quirk of the lips was all that was needed.

Kyle inhaled deeply, straightened, and wriggled on his chair. "Um ... I don't want everyone to freak out, but Gem, might be ... no, is ... pregnant."

Kara gasped and sat four inches taller.

Lexi's hands shot to her mouth.

Hunter choked on a mouthful of meat.

Gemma's skin turned a pasty pale shade of green.

My heart jolted against my ribs.

"But ..." Kyle raised his hand. "... it's not a good thing. It was an accident when we were on our getaway in the mountains. She forgot the pill, only to realize she'd left them at home after we'd done the deed a couple of times. We couldn't get to the drugstore because of the storm. We hoped the odds were in our favor, that it might not have happened. But we weren't lucky."

"Holy shit!" Hunter placed his hand on Gemma's arm. His brows pinched and his eyes hooded as if it hurt to breathe. "Why didn't you tell me . . . us?"

Gemma flicked her hair back over her shoulder and lifted her chin. She was one of the most resilient people I knew. "Of course we were going to tell you. We are now. I only peed on a stick yesterday. But I don't want to think about it. I don't want kids. We'll deal with it after New Year's."

Hunter clutched her hand. Concern quaked in his tone. "Are you okay?" He glanced at Kyle. "Bud?"

Kyle smiled but it didn't touch his eyes. "No. But we will be."

All eyes turned to Kara. She'd been obsessed with having kids for as long as I could remember.

"What?" Kara held her wine, hovering it halfway between her mouth and the table. "Why are you looking at me? I'm not the one who's pregnant. Just because I wanted children doesn't mean Gemma has to have them." She splayed her hand across her chest. "Gem, I know you. If this isn't what you want, you do what's right for you. I love you, and I'm here for you. Always."

But Kara couldn't hide the anguish in her eyes. She knocked back her wine, downing half the glass.

My heart ached for the girls. They both were strong women. Gemma was all about her career. Kara, who'd lost a baby and struggled through the surrogacy process, was all about children. But despite their differences, they loved and respected each other. That was what made my group of friends so phenomenal.

I placed my hand on Lexi's knee and gave it a gentle squeeze. I hoped we never had any issues having a family. Only time would tell.

Hunter clutched Gemma's hand again. "If you need anything, you just ask."

"Thanks, Hunt." Gemma waved at her untouched glass of wine. "What I would like is a fucking drink. But I feel so sick, I can't even face alcohol. If this is morning sickness, it sucks. It lasts all day."

"It's okay. I'll drink for you." Kyle downed his wine, grabbed Gemma's glass, and took a big gulp.

My heart cried for Gemma, but it bled for Kyle. He wanted

kids. He'd hinted at it several times over the past few months.

I grabbed the wine and topped up Kyle's glass. "I'm sorry you have to go through this."

"Don't be." Kyle stared at his drink. "Accidents happen. We all know that." He sucked in a deep breath and blinked the tears out of his eyes. "It's been a rough couple of days." He hooked his arm around Gemma's shoulders again, rubbed her arm, then kissed her temple. "But this is Gem's decision." He straightened in his chair. "We've talked about it. I'd love kids. But Gem's not ready, and she's all that matters."

"She certainly is." Lexi slumped in her seat; bewilderment still swirled in her eyes. "Life can throw some challenging curveballs, can't it? But guys, please know that we're here to support you. We'll be your shoulder to cry on. To have a drink with. To talk to. To listen. Whatever you need."

"Thanks, Lex. But we're good." Gemma ripped her bread roll open and slathered it with butter. "This will be over in two weeks."

"That gives you time to think about it, Gem." Hope tiptoed through Kara's tone. "You might change your mind."

"Nope. Not going to happen." Gemma stuffed a piece of bread into her mouth. "Can we please change the subject?"

"Maybe, not quite." I nudged Lexi's arm with my elbow and half-heartedly whispered in her ear, "Can I tell them our news?"

She glanced at Gemma, then at me. She pursed her lips and bobbed her head.

I turned to face my friends. "Now may not be the time, but it's as good as any . . . I think." I tilted my head to the side and wrinkled my nose at Gemma. "Sorry. No more baby talk after this, I promise. But Lex and I have decided to *have* a baby. We're gonna start trying."

"Arggggh!" Kara screamed, jumped to her feet, and rushed behind us. She bobbed down, hugged our shoulders and squeezed our heads against hers. "I'm so happy for you. Now this is exciting news."

"Chill, Kar." Lexi laughed as she peeled Kara's arms from

around her neck. "We literally only decided before, when we were feeding Ashleigh."

"That's so awesome." Kara dabbed tears from her eyes with the tips of her long fingernails and returned to her seat. She pulled in her chair and clapped her hands. "Yay! More babies."

Hunter half-stood and fist-pumped my hand across the table. "Fab news."

"So out of us three guys . . ." I teased as I picked up my wine glass and took a sip. "I'm the only one who has agreed to have a baby before knocking up my girl."

"Fuck you." Hunter chuckled. "We don't do things conventionally around here."

So true.

I caught sight of the distance in Gemma's eyes—Kyle's too. It must be hard to want different things. This would be a first for them. Gemma wouldn't be used to being the odd one out—her friends would all have children. She wouldn't. But she was tough and knew what she wanted in life. Her career and friends were everything to her. After coming from nothing, being an only child, and having a lonely upbringing in an unloving family, I understood her reasoning for not wanting kids probably better than most. I was an only child too. While my rough childhood had made me determined to provide a loving home for my future family, I guessed Gemma's past had turned her off from ever wanting children. Everyone was different.

On cue, Ashleigh cried in her rocker. Kara leaped from her chair, picked Ashleigh up, and brought her back to the table. Her tiny onesie-covered feet danced against Kara's thighs as Kara held her and kissed her on the cheek. "You think you're missing out on something exciting, don't you? You suffer from FOMO like your daddy?"

Dribble dripped from Ashleigh's tiny lips. Her cheeks were blotchy and red. Her long eyelashes were wet with tears. Supposedly, she was teething.

Kara goo-gooed and gah-gahhed at Ashleigh in her baby-talk

voice, ignoring her cries. "Uncle Hayds and Auntie Lex are going to have a baby soon, too. You're gonna have a playmate. Yippee!" She lifted Ashleigh above her head, then sat her in the crook of her arm. She let the baby suck and chew on her bangle. That shut Ashleigh up.

Cute.

Despite the interruption from Ashleigh, I couldn't contain my excitement. I smiled as I smoothed my hand over the back of Lexi's head and rubbed the base of her neck. "Lex will be an awesome mom. We can't wait."

Gemma smiled, but her eyes remained dull and distant. "Good luck, guys. I'm happy for you."

I mouthed to her, *"Sorry, Gem."*

She shook her head. "Don't be. If it's what you want, go for it."

Lexi wiped her fingers on her napkin, then smoothed her hand down my thigh. "It's scary and exciting. But we're ready."

"Absolutely. I'm gonna knock you up real good." I chuckled as I kissed her soft lips, then returned to eating my dinner.

This was certainly an unusual Christmas dinner, full of emotional ups and downs. My concern for Kyle and Gemma pressed against my chest, but I had to focus on my family. My future. With Lexi.

Having a baby would be the easy part. Convincing Lexi to move into a new apartment? Not so much. She hated letting go of anything sentimental. Before I got carried away, I'd best visit the bank, find out how much money we could borrow, and look at some condos for sale. We mightn't be able to afford a place of our own. But if we could, I would do everything in my power to convince Lexi that a new home was the right decision for our family.

It sounded easy. But nothing in life was simple.

But when it came to what was best for us, I was up for the challenge.

Chapter 5

KARA

In the middle of the crowded dance floor at The Knickerbocker Hotel for one of the hottest New Year's Eve events, my lips hovered an inch from Hunter's. We breathed in each other's air. With more celebrities and socialites than at a Grammys after-party dancing around us, my heart thudded in time with the loud, thumping music.

Hunter gyrated his body against mine with dance moves that bordered on being X-rated. It was one of the first nights I'd been out partying since Ashleigh had been born six months ago. I was in the mood to let my hair down. Hunter's hands on my body had my temperature approaching dangerous levels.

"Do you think we should tone it down?" I cupped his clean-shaven cheek. My voice, too breathy and hot.

"Never." His hand slid down my side, caught the edge of my thigh, and lifted my leg toward his hip. He rocked his pelvis into me, then swayed from side to side. He held me closer. Tighter. Dirty dancing was tame compared to this.

Oh, Lord.

If he kept grinding and rubbing his groin against me, there'd be trouble. The flimsy fabric of my party dress and silky panties didn't offer much protection against his hardened cock. His hands caressing my skin, the taste of whiskey on his lips, and the scent of his intoxicating citrusy cologne had ignited a fire in my belly. The few champagnes I'd drunk had shattered all traces of any inhibition. Hunter made every cell in my system quiver and made me feel like I was the sexiest woman alive. And he was quite intent on showing everyone that, too.

I glanced around the function room. All the guests wore elaborate bright-colored dresses or suits to celebrate Ivory Mink's Rainbow Ball. Everyone at the bar or outside on the rooftop balcony that overlooked Times Square was lost in conversation. They drank, partied with their friends, or danced up a storm in front of the DJ. No one paid much attention to us.

Good. Hunter was all mine. It was a nice change from being swarmed by fans or media, all desperate to meet my man.

Was there anywhere we could sneak off to and have a quickie? Sheer silver drapes hung over the windows. *Nope . . . not there.* The plush sofas and chairs scattered around the edges of the room were occupied. *Not an option.* Every nook and cranny in the bar was crowded. But Hunter was driving me wild. My want for him bordered on agony. It was too early to head home, wasn't it? Yes, it wasn't even midnight. Our babysitter was booked until three.

I tugged on the lapels of Hunter's bright orange dinner jacket. "Hunt?"

"Yeah?" A devilish glint lit his eyes.

"You wanna—"

"Yep."

Just as I was about to move, my friends caught my eye. Lexi and Hayden jumped around nearby, dancing with my sister, Naomi, and her husband, Anthony. But it was Kyle and Gemma who pulled me up short. Kyle had his arms wrapped around Gemma's petite frame; his cheek rested against the top of her head. Gemma cuddled against his chest. They swayed together, hardly moving in the middle of the jostling partygoers. They were in their own world, ignoring everyone around them.

I put my leg down and straightened my short skirt. The hot

buzz in my veins fizzled. Gemma had been so withdrawn since Christmas. The accidental pregnancy had wiped her vibrant energy.

"Pearl." Hunter caught the tip of my chin and turned my face toward him. His eyes flashed a warning. "Leave them alone. Gem doesn't need you on her case."

My heart ached. I loved how protective he was of Gemma and was hurt that he was right.

"I know." I'd had several conversations with Gemma since Christmas. Despite respecting Gemma's choice, I'd wanted her to consider having a baby for just one second. *One second.* But Gemma had stood her ground. She'd never wavered. She was adamant about not keeping the child. I admired her for being so strong. "I just want my feisty, ball-breaking Gem back."

He twirled me around, then caught me in his arms. "So do I. So don't make this harder on them than it already is."

"I'm not."

"You are." Hunter hooked his hands around my back and rested his forehead against mine. "In your subtle ways, you are. You're taking Ashleigh over to her place. Asking Gem to hold her. I don't miss a thing."

A small smile curved across my lips but then disappeared. My husband knew me too well. Maybe taking Ashleigh over to Gemma's house for a catch-up wasn't one of my finest moves. But I'd hoped Gemma watching Ashleigh play, or hugging and kissing her, might have woven *some* magic into Gemma's heart. The possibility was slim. I'd love everyone to have babies but knew that wasn't on Gemma's agenda. I should've been more considerate. "I'm sorry. I never meant to upset Gem. But my heart hurts for Kyle, too. He'd love to be a dad."

Hunter's eyes darkened. "He'll be okay. He'd do anything for Gem. But please don't wave our daughter like a carrot in front of Gem, okay?" His tone was soft but held an undercurrent of bite. "Not every person put on this planet wants a family. I was like that, too. Remember?"

He shuffled me sideways to avoid a bunch of partygoers dashing onto the dance floor, then he spun me around and we continued to dance.

Four years ago, when I'd become pregnant with Ryan, Hunter had been against keeping the baby. But he'd come around. Even after our loss.

He splayed one hand across the small of my back and tugged me closer. With his other hand, he connected our palms, entwined our fingers, and slowly waltzed me in time with the music. "Kar, you need to focus on us. Our family. We have an amazing daughter to love and cherish. I count my blessings every day that I have both of you in my life."

The tension dissipated in my shoulders. "You're right. I am grateful. And happy. We have so much good in our lives."

The days since Ashleigh was born had been the best days of my life. Being a mom came to me as naturally as breathing. Being a wife and having an incredible husband and a beautiful home had exceeded my dreams. Now, in the year ahead, new plans would take shape. In February, I'd begin part-time work at Ivory Mink's Fashion House. I'd have my premier limited collection and showing in the first week of September at a Pre-Fashion Week spectacular.

Funny how perspectives changed. After I'd desperately wanted nothing more than to have a child and be a mom, once Ashleigh was about a month old, I'd yearned to return to work. My desire to design again had simmered beneath the surface for so long, but Hunter had brought it out of me. My love and passion for design had hit with a vengeance. I'd been adamant about being a full-time mother, but my priorities had altered. With both of us working on new projects, Hunter and I had hired a nanny two months ago. Finding Diego through a friend of Ivory's was meant to be.

Life was about balance.

We worked hard at it.

I'd overcome my health issues—physical and mental—thanks

to therapy, and the unrelenting support and love from my amazing friends and husband. I had landed in a great place. Life couldn't get much better.

I had changed.

Maybe there was hope for Gemma? No . . . I loved Gemma just the way she was.

And I loved my husband. I cupped Hunter's cheek. "I love you. Always remember that."

"And I love you." His tone dripped with renewed fiery hunger. His gaze turned smoldering hot—hot enough to burn my panties. "Where were we before we got sidetracked?"

My gaze fell to his lips. His citrusy cologne filled my head. My heart jumped to the DJ's throbbing loud beat. What had we been talking about?

Hunter pressed his mouth to mine, parted his lips, and flicked his tongue against mine, all hot and delicious. No one had ever made me feel like this. All wicked, wild, and wanton.

"Hey?" Naomi hollered over the booming music. She clutched my shoulder and dragged me away from Hunter. "You two need to book a room."

Yes. I agreed. We should've stayed here at the hotel for the night. But I didn't want to be away from Ashleigh that long.

"This is so much fun," Naomi squealed as she raised her near-full flute of champagne in the air, elbowing Anthony in the chin as she lifted her arms.

"Yeah. Great." He rubbed his jaw. His tone was loaded with sarcasm but creases formed at the corners of his eyes as he laughed.

"Enjoying the Moët?" I giggled as I gave Naomi a quick hug.

"Hell yeah." She swayed on her feet. "Last year, I was pregnant with Ashleigh, so I'm making up for it now."

"I see that." Hunter caught Naomi's arm to steady her. Anthony did the same on her other side.

"Is Diego babysitting Ashleigh?" Naomi pouted.

"He certainly is." I bobbed my head. "He's awesome."

"Kar refused to let me hire a female nanny." Hunter's eyes shimmered as he pulled my hip against his side. "My wife still doesn't trust me."

"I do." I gave Hunter a saucy grin. "But I won't put anything tempting in front of you if I can avoid it."

He narrowed his gaze. "Hmm. Maybe I should be worried about you and Diego?"

"God, no." I wrinkled my nose. "He's too short." I liked my men tall, like Hunter. But I had to admit, Diego, with his gorgeous, tanned skin, Venezuelan accent, and dark brown eyes and hair, wasn't hard on the eye. But I was convinced that Hunter was more his type.

"Can we invite ourselves over for dinner next week so we can see Ashleigh?" Naomi threaded her arm around Anthony's middle and rested her head against his shoulder. "We haven't seen her since before Christmas."

"Sure." I rubbed my sister's arm. Naomi had a special bond with Ashleigh after being her surrogate. I could never thank her enough for what she'd done for Hunter and me. "How's Thursday? We're busy until then."

"Oh . . . that long?" Naomi winced and rubbed her brow.

But then she glanced at Anthony, and my skin prickled. *Oh, shit. What had happened now?* My sister was no good at hiding news.

Anthony chuckled and shook his head. "Just go for it, Nae. It'll kill you otherwise."

"Nae? What is it?" I gripped onto the back of Hunter's jacket to steady myself.

Naomi downed her flute and placed it on a passing waiter's tray. "I'm no good at keeping decisions under wraps. Don't ever tell me your secrets because I'll blurt them across Manhattan." She smiled, took a deep breath, and smoothed her hands over the hipline of her bright blue cocktail dress. "I may be totally crazy. Anthony certainly thinks I am. I know this isn't the right time or place to bring this up, but I'm drunk, and I don't care."

"Bring up what?" Hunter jerked his chin at Naomi. He was just as impatient as I was.

Naomi grabbed my hand. A smile as bright as the Times Square Ball lit her face. "I was wondering . . . if you wanted to have another baby. You have one frozen embryo left, right? I'd like to be your surrogate again. If you'll have me."

The air shot out of my lungs. My head spun. My heartbeat thundered in my throat. "You *what?* Are you serious? Or is this drunk talk?"

"Nae?" Hunter wiped his hand over his face. The color had drained from his cheeks. "Holy shit. That's amazing, but we can't ask that of you. Not again."

"You're not asking. I'm offering." Naomi staggered back a step and hit a guy dancing behind her. "Sorry." She held up her hands, then turned back to us. She straightened her shoulders and laughed. "Fuuuuck. I've drunk a lot." But then seriousness washed over her face. "We lost two embryos before Ashleigh. This may not work. But I want to try."

"Anthony?" Shock quaked in Hunter's voice. "Are you okay with this?"

"Hunter, we've both married hell-bent Knight women." He hooked his arm around Naomi's shoulders and planted a kiss on the side of her head. "We've talked about it. I won't deny that I think it's too soon, but . . . as long as *we* don't have another kid, I'm okay with it."

"Good thing we only have one embryo left, right?" Hunter half chuckled, half smirked.

"Yes, indeed." Anthony downed the remains of his wine. "I'd like my wife to stop being a baby oven after this."

"Nae?" My head still spiraled like a turntable. "You went through so much with Ashleigh and the miscarriages. Are you sure you want to do this?"

"Yes." There was no doubt in my sister's voice. "I loooove being pregnant. I know how happy you are with Ashleigh and know how much you wanted a bunch of kids. Don't you want to take the chance? See if you can have another?"

Hunter threaded his fingers through his long hair and clutched a handful against his scalp. Was he lost for words like I was?

I couldn't breathe. *Another baby?*

This was huge.

I'd always wanted three or four kids, but after our losses, I was grateful I finally had one happy, healthy, beautiful, biological daughter. But our remaining frozen embryo had lingered in the back of my mind. I'd never imagined Naomi would volunteer to be a surrogate again. It was too much. Too incredible. Too insane . . . Too perfect. Tears welled in my eyes. "Nae, really?"

Lexi and Hayden wove through the crowd toward us, their hands full of shots. They edged their way into our little group and handed around glasses of something that looked and smelled like coffee liqueur.

"You guys are being too serious for people at a New Year's Eve party." Lexi placed a drink in my hand. "Get this shit into you."

Hayden dragged Kyle and Gemma out of their huddle to join us and placed glasses in their hands. Gemma just handed hers to Kyle. Even though Gemma had no plans to keep her baby, she hadn't been drinking. That kept my glimmer of hope alive. Hope that something was gnawing away in the deep, dark recesses of her mind.

We formed a tight circle and held our shots together.

Hayden raised his glass. "Here's to an incredible new year. Cheers. Woohoo!" He downed his shot in one gulp, as did everyone else. Gemma forced a smile and threw her hand up in the air. There was a spark of life inside her after all. I couldn't wait until the old life-of-the-party Gemma returned.

Hayden was definitely liquored up and having a great time. Lexi was right there with him.

Pressed together in the middle of the crowded dance floor, I danced with my friends. As I licked the coffee liqueur off my lips, my mind hurtled back to Naomi. The chance to have another baby skipped around inside my head and flickered through my heart.

Thoughts of a baby overruled everything, even having a quickie with Hunter.

He caught me around the waist. His lips hovered near my ear. "I can tell you're thinking about it. So, what do you reckon?"

I quirked an eyebrow. "About the quickie or a baby?"

"Both . . . but a baby."

My head spun as I placed my hand on his chest. His heart raced beneath my touch. "I'm amazed we have Ashleigh. But having another baby? That would be incredible. I know there's a risk, and it may amount to nothing . . . but what if it works?"

"Having a little brother or sister for Ashleigh would be cool."

"So . . ." Excitement filled my chest. "If Naomi still feels the same way when she's sober, are you up for this? Another baby?"

Hunter's azure eyes glinted as he nodded. "Yeah. I am."

I flung my arms around his neck and kissed him hard. He picked me up and twirled me around, then placed me back on my feet.

"So, is that a 'yes?'" Naomi hollered from beside me.

I spun to face her. Tears pricked my eyes. "Yes. Oh my God, yes." I threw my arms around Naomi and hugged her.

"What's 'yes?'" Gemma's tone was laden with caution. Concern rippled through her emerald eyes.

My stomach somersaulted, cartwheeled, and backflipped. I couldn't contain my excitement. "Nae wants to be our surrogate again." I clutched Gemma's and Lexi's hands and jumped up and down. "We're gonna try for another baby."

"Oh, wow!" Lexi screamed and hugged me. "That's amazing."

Congratulations zoomed around my group of friends. Hayden swiped another round of shots from a waiter who walked past, but Gemma opted for an orange juice.

Raising her glass, Gemma led the toast. "Well . . . here's to new babies, and in my case, no fucking babies. Cheers!"

Kyle downed his drink, tossed his plastic shot glass onto the floor, and pulled Gemma into his arms. I hadn't seen him drink this much in years.

As he dipped his head and nuzzled against Gemma's ear, I heard him mutter, "I love you. That's all that matters."

Hunter slapped Kyle on the back, then turned to me. His concern morphed into a radiant smile. He swept me into his embrace, twirled me around, and continued to dance.

Everyone joined in, swaying their arms in the air, and jumping in time with the music.

Hunter's eyes blazed bright as he dipped me backward. "I can't believe it. Another baby?"

"Let's hope it works." We'd learned not to get our hopes up. All I could do was pray. I caressed his cheek, his skin smooth beneath my touch. "I love you."

"Love you too, my beautiful Pearl."

"Everybody," the DJ hollered. "Are you ready?" He pointed outside through the huge glass windows to the Time Square Ball glowing in the near distance. "Let's go."

The ball dropped slowly.

The partygoers counted down.

"Ten. Nine. Eight. Seven. Six. Five. Four. Three. Two. One. Happy New Year!"

Party poppers popped. Streamers exploded. Champagne overflowed from glasses. Cheers rang throughout the room. But I just wrapped my arms around Hunter's shoulders and kissed him slowly, deeply, tenderly, projecting all the love I had in my heart toward him.

Trying for another baby might not work. The odds weren't good. Our last attempt may fail. But leaving one embryo frozen hadn't given me closure. This would. One way or another, we'd know if we could have another biological child. This was our last chance. Our only hope. We had to take the plunge.

Chapter 6

KYLE

"Here you are." Hunter barged into my home music room without knocking.

I half-smirked, took a sip of my JD, then placed the glass on top of the digital piano. "Was I supposed to be somewhere else?"

Had Gemma and I forgotten a meeting? A function? A dinner? There hadn't been anything in my calendar. *Had there?* My mind had been preoccupied lately. But after tomorrow, my head would be clear. After I took Gemma to the clinic, our *little mishap* would be behind us.

Fuck.

I didn't want Gemma to go through with it, but I had no other choice.

"Um . . . no. I just came to check on you." Hunter dropped his bag of groceries by the door, then shrugged off his anorak and dropped it beside them. He grabbed the office chair from behind the desk, wheeled it across the floor, and took a seat near me. "Where's Gem?"

"Having a shower."

Hunter's eyes glinted as he arched one eyebrow. "And you're not with her?"

I puffed air through my nose. "Um . . . no. Not tonight." I

grabbed the bottle of JD and topped up my glass. "I just needed a moment alone." I'd never thought I'd need time out from Gemma, but I needed to find a way to keep a grip on my emotions. I picked up my drink and took a swig. "I needed some liquid strength for tomorrow. You want one?"

"Nah. I'm good." Hunter leaned forward and rested his elbows on his knees. The concern in his eyes snagged my heart. "Do you want me to come with you to the clinic?"

I shook my head. If I moved any other part of my body, my heart ached too much. No matter what I'd said, no matter how much I'd put my case forward, Gemma hadn't changed her mind. I loved her and would support her, but that didn't mean her decision didn't hurt like fucking hell.

"No. I'll be fine." I would be. Just not yet.

"How's Gem?"

"Nervous. Anxious. Terrified. She wants this over and done with."

Two weeks ago, just after New Year's, I'd taken Gemma to our doctor. Concerned about our busy schedule and her recent health issues, Gemma had opted for a surgical rather than medical termination. My gut hurt at the thought of either option. Tomorrow it'd all be over.

Hunter jutted his chin at me. "What are you doing in front of the piano? You haven't played that in months."

Guitars and drums were my go-to instruments, but I didn't mind sitting behind the keys every now and then. Gemma and Hunter were much better players. They could get more out of the piano than I ever could.

"I was just thinking about Mom." My fingers flowed over the keys, tinkering out Beethoven's *Für Elise*. It had been one of Mom's favorite pieces of music. "Mom loved teaching you and Gem to play. After Emily died, Mom loved Gem like she was her own daughter. You were always like another son. My family."

"Yeah. Your mom was awesome." Hunter bobbed his head, then tucked his long hair behind his ear. "So, what is this? Are you having a pity party? About Gemma not wanting to be a mom?"

"Fuck no." *Kinda.* "I'm just mentally preparing. You know that moment before you go on stage, when you close your eyes, focus, clear your head, and pray everything will go to plan? That everything will be okay? That's all I'm doing."

"Bud, I'm sorry Gem's decision isn't what you wanted." He wheeled his chair two feet closer. "You have every right to be upset, angry, disappointed, and frustrated. I feel for you, because I know what you're going through. I've been through it."

"This is different from you and Kar."

"No, it's not. You're at a total loss. You feel powerless. No matter what you say or feel or want, it doesn't matter because it's up to the girl to decide."

Shit. He knew. He was right. "It just sucks." I dragged my hand down my face. I wanted it to wipe away my fatigue, but it didn't work. "I won't deny it. But I'd never want Gem to do anything she didn't want to do. We'll get over this. Move on. Make new music. Like we always do." So why wouldn't my heart stop shuddering in pain?

"Then why are you sitting here getting drunk?"

"I'm coping." I smirked, then knocked back another mouthful of JD.

"Imagine what Gem's going through. This hasn't been easy for her." Deep furrows drilled into Hunter's brow as if he felt every ounce of her pain and anguish. "This has gutted her. She's processed this in her own way. You know her better than anyone else. She projects this stoic front, but on the inside, she's mulled over every option, weighed out the pros and cons, contemplated every what-if. Not having you on her side throughout this issue would be devastating her."

Hunter's tone twisted my guts into knots. "I'm not blind. This honestly feels like the first time we haven't agreed on something." *Not including our wedding.*

"It has been weird." Hunter picked up Gemma's acoustic guitar and plucked the strings. "But I love her too. I will until the day I die. She is everything. We have this amazing life because of her. She has kept us together, built us up, been our strength. Now she needs you to help her through probably the toughest decision she's ever had to make in her life. She's no doubt tortured herself thinking she's as selfish, unloving, and unmaternal as her mom. She's loathed Janine for those things."

Hunter struck some low chords. Each one reverberated deep in my chest. Gemma was nothing like her mother. She put everyone before herself. She didn't chase after or marry men for their money. She'd never betrayed someone she loved.

"But having a baby terrifies her." Hunter's tone softened. "Not just because she thinks it will mess with our music and thinks she doesn't have the capacity to love your child; she's worried about losing you. She's afraid having a family will destroy what you have, and you'll leave, like her dad did. You're the non-negotiable element."

Shit. This *was* about her dad. "But we've talked about that."

"Doesn't matter." Hunter strummed downward on the guitar's strings, then cut the sound off with a slap of his hand. "Regardless of how crappy and shitty you feel, times that by a million and that's what she's going through. For her, there is only one option. It doesn't mean it's been an easy choice to make."

I sniffled and rubbed the tip of my nose with my fingertips. "I know. I feel her. She doesn't have to say anything because I can see it in her eyes. Feel it in the way she holds me, touches me." I splayed my hand across my chest and clutched my hoodie. "But it doesn't have to be a choice. I love her. I'm there for her. I've told her a million times I'm not going anywhere. My love for her is and will never be in question."

"She won't ever put that at risk. She'll always choose you."

My heart faltered. Closing my eyes, I absorbed the weight of Hunter's words. *She chooses me over anything and everything else.* I lowered my head and softened my tone. "Yeah. That's pretty wicked, right?

Her love was true and unwavering. Profound and intense. My

love for her was unbreakable. But she was afraid I'd leave? That would never happen. I raked my fingers through my hair. Was there anything I could do to reassure her?

Maybe some old wounds ran too deep.

Nothing I'd said or done had healed the scars her shitty parents had caused. That snagged my heart, but it would never crack or splinter my devotion to her. Slouching my shoulders, I rubbed my chest. "After tomorrow . . . I may never have the chance to have a family again. Accepting that has been hard. I'd hoped she would come around, give some hint that it might happen in the future, but I'm not sure it ever will."

"Is that an issue for you?" Fear darkened Hunter's eyes. "Will it affect your future together?"

"God, no." How could Hunter even think that? That wasn't an option.

"Good." Hunter let out a deep breath. "Don't scare me like that. You two mean too much to me." He rested his arm on top of the guitar. "I know this isn't the outcome you wanted, and putting it behind you will be hard. But you will. Look at Kar and me. We've been on a Dakar Rally, not a *Driving Miss Daisy* kind of relationship. I like to think that somehow we would've ended up together regardless of the route we'd taken. If she hadn't kept Ryan, we would've eventually gotten together and fucked around behind your backs until we were caught or had fallen for each other. But we wouldn't have had Ryan, and we wouldn't have had Ashleigh, or the chance to have another biological child. We would've adopted or gone down some other path to have kids. But that's our road map, not yours."

I followed Hunter's gaze to the framed photo of the three of us winning the Discovered-On-YouTube contest hanging on the wall. We looked so young eleven years ago. Hunter, with his head full of short wavy curls. Gemma with stars in her eyes. Me, skinny as a rake, before I'd toned up and filled out.

Hunter's eyebrows pinched together as if too many memories bombarded him all at once. "We've been through so much. What you and Gem are going through is just a bump in the road. You've been across your own treacherous terrain. Whatever valley you are in, or crossroads you face, you will always end up on top of a mountain. You belong together. She may never want kids. So emerge from this stronger, find new ways to grow together, love each other, and leave your mark on the world as an incredible united front. Your love will defy any lifetime."

Tears prickled my eyes, but I blinked them away. *Be strong. For Gem.* "Thanks, man." I rubbed my palms against my thighs. "I know you love us. We'll be okay. Nothing, not even this, will break us." I raised my hands, glided my fingers over the piano keys, then burst out chuckling. "But I did just come down here for a drink."

"Fuck you." Hunter rolled forward and punched my arm.

"Ow!" I rubbed my bicep. That was a bit more than a play-punch. "I thought I was the deep, moody one. What was with all the road references and mountains and shit? You need to write a song? Work on new music?"

Hunter punched my arm again, then rolled back to be out of my reach. "You can joke all you like. But I know you. I love that you're being strong for Gem when I know you're not feeling it. But I feel for her, too. That's all."

"Yeah." I lowered my gaze and stared at my gold wedding ring. I worried about her more than myself. I'd love her for all eternity.

"Did you catch up with Bec and the others today?" Hunter asked. "How were their vacations? Sorry Kar and I couldn't be there."

"Don't be." I took another sip of my JD. "Visiting lawyers to draw up a new surrogacy agreement for Naomi was more important than being there when I told them about Gem."

"Maybe. But, man . . . " Hunter's tone turned light and playful. "I wanted to see the look on Bec's face when you told her. What did she say?"

When we'd broken the news to our personal assistant and management team, they'd been just as shocked as our friends had been. "Bec thought we were joking at first—thought she was being punk'd. But when she realized we were serious, she was more dumbstruck than a school nerd being asked to prom by the head cheerleader. She said we should've called her. She would've called in the US Army to get Gem the pill when we were stuck in the snow. Bec is good, but not that good."

Hunter quirked his lip. "I wouldn't put anything past Bec."

Bec was the most incredible PA. She'd always saved our asses, put up with our shit, produced the odd miracle, and managed our lives, our fans, and our travel without question. She complained, argued, and cursed more than Samuel L. Jackson on screen, but that made her so much fun. She'd always kept us grounded. The best thing was, when we'd paid her a Christmas bonus, she'd signed up to work with us for another five years. She never planned on leaving Everhide.

"Yeah, well." I stabbed some low chords on the piano keys. I should've called her. *Damn it.* "We didn't."

"What about Kate and Sophie?"

"Kate panicked and prepared a press release in case someone sees us at the clinic. Sophie was just ecstatic that our appearances and album plans won't be affected."

"Gem will be happy about that too." Hunter grabbed my glass and downed a mouthful. He still didn't drink much after his vocal cord surgery.

"Same. We're all about the music." But my heart didn't feel it right then. I wanted more. More with Gemma.

"That we are." Hunter slapped his hand on his thigh. "So . . . if you ever want your fix of kids, come over and play with Ashleigh. We hope to have a new addition by the end of the year—so do Hayden and Lexi. There will be plenty of babies for you to love. We're family; remember that. We're thicker than blood."

"Thanks, man."

Hunter's cell phone buzzed. He jumped off the chair and grabbed it out of his anorak. He swiped and read the screen. "Shit. I gotta go. It's Ashleigh's feed-time and I have the formula. I dropped a whole can of this crap on the floor before."

"Okay. Thanks for checking on us."

"Anytime." He swiped his coat and grocery bag off the floor and opened the music room door. "I'll just run up and wish Gem luck for tomorrow, then see myself out."

"Go for it. I'll call you tomorrow . . . after. Maybe in the evening sometime."

"Don't sweat it. Gem will need you."

As the door shut behind Hunter, I turned to the piano and played my mom's favorite tune. Images of my family swirled through my head. Playing on the beach with my sister. Mom singing at church. My dad sitting in his armchair, watching sports and drinking beer. But as I'd gotten older, the memories had faded. I couldn't remember the color of Emily's dresses. Or recall the feel of my mom's hugs. Even the strikes of my dad's hand seemed not to sting as much. But then . . . fresh, vibrant, radiant images of Gemma filled my mind. Her laugh, her kisses, her music. Her standing before me in her wedding dress, promising to love me forever. She would always be enough. She was my family. My life.

I downed another drink. Once Hunter had left, I drew in a deep breath, stuffed my hurt deep down in my heart, and locked it away. I closed the piano, turned off the lights, and headed upstairs.

My love for Gemma was higher than any mountain—it was bigger than the universe. I'd step out of this rugged valley tomorrow and hit a new trail running. But tonight, I'd hold Gemma in my arms. Pray tomorrow held no issues. And most of all, I'd be there for her. I'd always be hers . . . the man, the strength, and all the love she ever needed. I'd never be like her dad.

Bring on tomorrow, so we could put this mishap behind us.

Chapter 7

KYLE

The following morning, I sat on the sofa waiting for Gemma to come downstairs. A lump of lead lay in the pit of my stomach. A dull ache lingered in my heart and head. I'd hardly slept. Gemma had tossed and turned all night. Neither of us was looking forward to today. Resting my elbows on my knees, I stared at the half-burned candle on the coffee table.

Today, we'd put an end to Gemma's unwanted pregnancy.

I'd never had that twinge, that pull inside my soul, that tug in my heart or desire to have my own children until Hunter's daughter Ashleigh was born. Now I could picture Gemma and me with our own child as clear as a video clip—our kid running around our home, dressed in a rockin' romper suit, slamming on the piano keys and banging on the drums.

But it wasn't meant to be.

Fuck.

Footsteps padded down the wooden staircase and headed toward me.

I wiped my eyes with my fingertips, glanced up and summoned a fake smile. Gemma's emerald eyes held no glint, her cheeks had lost their rosiness, and her hair hung limp and loose around her shoulders. Being pregnant for the past few weeks had swallowed her soul. I wanted my Gemma back.

"You ready?" She swept her hand across my shoulders.

"No. You?"

"Yep. Let's get this over and done with."

Gemma took a step toward the door, but I caught her hand and tugged her to sit beside me. Swiveling to face her, I entwined our fingers. "Gem." My voice caught in my dry throat. "Are you sure about this?"

"Yes. One hundred percent." Her tone was cold as the Arctic. It held not one amp of emotion.

She'd never wavered from her hard no about having a baby from the start. A year ago, I would've said the same thing. But life had changed. I had to fight for what I wanted one last time. Before it was too late.

"I'd love to have a family with you."

"We've talked about this." She withdrew her hand and rubbed her thighs. "You married the wrong girl if you want kids."

"No. Never. I love you so fucking much. You hear me?" Desperation edged into my voice. I was at the end of the gangplank, on the brink of falling. If I hit the water, the battle would be over. Was there anything else I could say to change her mind? To convince her I was with her for life? "We've been through so much together, so many good times and bad. We have survived and keep getting stronger." I pulled the neckline of my sweatshirt down my chest. "I have your name tattooed in a tulip on my heart. I declared my love for you in front of the universe the day we got married. I swear on my life, no matter how hard things get, I promise I will never leave you."

Pain rippled across her face.

"We have so much love for each other—it is impossible for our child not to be loved." I softened my tone. "We can do this. We can have a family."

She swayed and shook her head. "No . . . we can't."

I clawed my brain for other options. Our family of friends pummeled my mind. "But Kar and Hunt have a baby. Hopefully they'll have another child soon. Lexi and Hayden are trying. This is perfect timing. We could raise our families together."

"Kyle. Please. Stop." Tears welled in her eyes. "I love you and our life too much. I don't want it to change."

"I love music just as much as you do. We have an incredible life. It's fucking awesome. But we could tone down our schedule. Take more time to write an album. Stretch out recording sessions. Spread out tour legs and take breaks. We could adjust for a child. Be a family."

"I have all the family I need."

"But you adore Ashleigh. Why not our own baby?"

She winced, closed her eyes and lowered her chin. "I love Ashleigh. She's gorgeous. But I can give her back at the end of the day." A tear fell, catching on the edge of her cheek. "Kyle, I'm sorry. Everyone has been supportive and understanding. Especially you. I know you want this. You've tried to sway my decision. I've contemplated every outcome. I've talked to you about it until I've gone hoarse. But nothing has changed. It's not just about you or my parents and upbringing. It's about me. *I* don't want a baby. Please don't make this harder than it already is."

I placed my hand on her knee and gave it a gentle squeeze. "I'm sorry. I don't want to upset you. But this sucks. Having a baby would be incredible. You'd be a kickass mom. But I have to . . . and by God, I do, I will stand by your decision. Because I love you, no matter what. Maybe this time in our lives isn't right. I hope that one day, maybe in a few years, it will be."

A baby would mean the world to me. I'd hoped I'd opened her mind to the possibility of having a family in the not-too-distant future. But by the stone set in her face, it'd never happen.

"Please don't bet on it." She wiped a tear from her cheek and rose to her feet. "Come on. Let's go. I don't want to be late."

At the private clinic, as Gemma filled out the paperwork and consent forms, I slumped on the sofa beside her. My vision blurred as I focused on nothing. Not the TV. Not the coffee table stacked with old gossip magazines. Not the other unoccupied chairs. My heart didn't want to beat. Why did I feel so awful when I loved Gemma so much? Deep down, I understood and respected her decision. It was her body. But was the pain in my heart the fear of knowing that this was as close as I'd ever come to being a father? *Yep.*

Gemma leaped to her feet and handed the clipboard of forms back to the receptionist.

"Thank you. Please take a seat, Mrs. McIntyre." The receptionist, wearing caked-on makeup and long fake eyelashes, waved her pointy pink fingernail toward the sofa where I sat. "The doctor will be with you shortly."

Gemma returned to sit beside me and curled against my arm. I drew her into my embrace and kissed the top of her head. But the slight tremor in her touch and tension in her grip didn't go unnoticed.

My heart sank to the floor, but I stitched on a brave mask. "Hey, precious. You've got this." As I rubbed her arm, I closed my eyes to ward off the tears lurking behind my eyes. "I love you. I love you with every fiber in my body. We'll put this behind us. Move on. It'll be like nothing ever happened."

But a piece of my heart would never be the same.

I let out a slow breath. Inside, my chest shuddered. The ache meandered through my veins, and anguish wrapped around my bones. I squeezed my eyes shut and sniffled. *Fuck.* I actually sniffled.

A nurse in pale pink scrubs came into the waiting room. "Mrs. McIntyre? We're ready for you."

"Here goes nothing." Gemma gave me a quick kiss on the cheek, then stood.

She wiped her hands on the back of her jeans and took a step toward the nurse, but I reached out to halt her. I rose to my feet, drove my hands into her hair and kissed her lips. I hugged her tight. I didn't want to let her go. This was the only way I could say goodbye to the baby I'd never gotten to know.

Fuck. Why was this so hard?

"Hey?" She tapped me on the back and pulled out of my embrace. "I've gotta go."

"I'll be here." I squeezed her hand before I released my hold. "Always."

She stepped backward. Tears pooled on the rims of her eyes. "I love you. I'll be back soon."

In forty-five minutes, this would be behind us.

"I love you, too." I blew her a kiss, then stuffed my hands in my pockets to hide the shake.

Gemma spun on her heels and headed toward the procedure room.

Fuck.

I slumped onto the sofa and let my head fall back. I covered my eyes with my palms and rubbed them. There was no turning back now. What was done was done.

I watched the clock on the wall. Each minute that passed was raw agony.

Five minutes. Ten minutes. Fifteen minutes.

My heart cried. Was Gemma okay? Would this hurt?

As I stared at the small window, pain rippled through my chest. Words and music battered my head. *Shit!* Now wasn't the time to be bombarded by a song. But it boomed and blared and beat inside my skull like I was at a live rock concert. I wiped my eyes on my shirtsleeve, ripped out my cell phone from my jacket draped on the chair beside me and typed madly.

> *Sorry I didn't get the chance to know you*
> *Sorry I didn't get to hear your laugh*
> *One more time*
> *Now you've gone and left me all alone*
> *No words can explain the hole left in my heart*
> *I should've told you that I loved you*
> *Should've told you I never wanted to part*
> *One more time*
> *Sorry my words were not enough*
> *Sorry I didn't get to hold you in my arms*

I should've fought to hold on to you longer
Together, I know we would've been stronger
Then you might not have walked away
Because believe me baby, baby
All I wanted was . . . for you to . . . stay

Forty minutes. Fifty minutes. An hour.

I glanced at the double doors. What the fuck was taking so long?

Had something gone wrong?

Shit.

Panic crept into my heart. My palms turned clammy. After another fifteen excruciating minutes, I walked up to the receptionist. "Excuse me . . . but is Gem okay? It's taking longer than expected."

We'd had enough medical dramas to last a lifetime. We didn't need any more.

"I'll go check for you." The receptionist waddled off through the swinging doors and returned a few minutes later.

Gemma and the nurse walked behind her.

I rushed toward Gemma. She collapsed into my arms, crying.

The tears looming at the back of my eyes stung like acid. "Shh. I got you, babe. I got you."

As I rested my head on top of hers and stroked her long dark brown hair, a lone tear slid down my cheek. Holding her tight, I let her cry as much as she needed to.

"I'll leave you for a few moments." The nurse smiled softly and headed out through the doors.

Gemma sobbed. That wasn't like her, but she'd just been through a traumatic experience. Her tears soaked through to my skin and burned against my aching heart. I hugged her tighter, giving her what she needed—my love, my heart, and every ounce of strength I had left.

"I . . . I . . . I—" Her voice muffled against my sweatshirt.

"What was that?"

She looked up at me. Tears streamed down her cheeks. "I

went in there, and I kept thinking about you, how much you love me, and how you've done everything for me. How happy we are and how good our life is. I love you, and would do anything for you, and I always want to show you how much you mean to me. You have changed my life for the better. You are my soulmate, my love, my everything."

I caught the tops of her arms. "I know that, Gem. We'll always have each other."

She blubbered and shook her head. "I know you wanted this."

"Yeah, but it wasn't meant to be."

Her chin quivered. "I'm terrified."

"Of what? I'm not going anywhere. It's over."

"No. It's not." She shook her head. "I . . . I couldn't do it."

My heart thudded a thousand beats per second. My ears rang. "You what?"

"It's still in me."

"You didn't . . . holy shit." A fevered rush shot over my skin. "Holy *fucking shit.* You mean?"

"I don't think I'll ever change." She struggled to talk over her weeping. "I don't think that *need* inside of me to have a baby will ever change. But I don't want you to regret not having one. Or to resent me. We're not our parents. We prove that every day. Our love is so strong. We struggle to breathe when we're not in the same room. When I'm with you, I can do anything. Together, *we* can do anything. Even have a family. I'm doing this for *us.* Because I love you. So fucking much."

"You mean . . . we're gonna have a baby?"

Tears cascaded down her cheeks as she nodded.

I drew her against my chest, caressed her damp face and kissed her. Kissed her hard. Kissed her lips, her cheeks, her forehead. I wiped away her beautiful tears. "Oh, Gem. I could never resent you. Not in a million years. Are you sure about this?"

"No."

"What . . . what changed your mind?"

"You. You never gave up on me. You never got mad or angry.

You just loved and reassured me, even though not having the baby broke your heart. You stand by me all the time." She clutched the front of my shirt and gave it a little tug. "Everything you and our friends said or did chiseled away at my resolve. But I'm stubborn. I didn't want to listen to the arguments going on inside my head. Then, this morning, when you pointed to my name tattooed on your heart, I nearly caved. I see it every day, but I forgot the weight of what it means. It's the same reason your name is inked onto my arm." She twisted her elbow toward me; but my name branded on the inside of her bicep was hidden beneath her hoodie. "When I was sitting in the procedure room, I just stared at my wedding ring, recalling the vows we'd made to each other. I am yours, and you are mine. We're permanent. Always and forever."

"Always." I trembled all over. My knees threatened to buckle. "Now I'm freaking out. I wanted this, but I never thought it would happen."

"Well, you better fucking want it, because I'm still pregnant."

"Say that again."

"Don't push it."

"Oh. My. God." I threw back my head as I laughed and cried happy tears. Finding a smidgen of composure, I stared down at her and caressed her gorgeous face. "There are not enough words to describe how much I love you. I can't believe this. We're gonna have a baby?"

"Uh-huh."

"*Yes!*" I picked her up and spun her around. My heart soared through the clouds. "This is so incredible. Thank you."

This moment was just as magical as the first time she'd kissed me on the deck at the beach house, and the first time she'd said she loved me, and the day she'd asked me to marry her, and the day she'd said 'I do' in Belize. Now . . . a baby. *Wow!* Life certainly had taken a very unexpected turn. But it was one I was ready for. Gemma had just made me the happiest man alive. Again.

Chapter 8

GEMMA

Where the hell am I? Blindfolded, I took cautious steps as Kara and Lexi held my hands and guided me forward. My breathing and heart rate had quickened. After being kidnapped, I no longer liked the dark and not being free to move. Even though I trusted these two girls with my life, my pulse pounded like a drum. Diego, Kara's nanny, shuffled somewhere nearby, cooing at Ashleigh. Chester, my bodyguard, was close by; I could smell his cologne. The drive here—wherever here was—had been short, so we weren't far from home. "When are you going to tell me what's going on, or do I just pull off this stupid eye mask? You know I hate surprises."

"Have faith." Kara hugged my arm tighter. "We've got you, but we know this surprise is just what you need."

"I don't *need* anything." *Breathe. I'm okay.*

"Yeah. You do." Lexi patted my other arm, then let go.

Metal hinges grated and scraped, like the opening of a heavy door.

Shit. Where the hell have they brought me?

As they led me inside, warm heat hit my face—a welcomed relief from the outside chill and late January snow. But my other senses were in overdrive. My skin prickled—the space felt *big*. My ears homed in on the soft music played nearby. *Olivia Rodrigo.* My nostrils tingled—a subtle hint of fruity perfume lingered in the air. *Carla?*

My friends steered me across the concrete floor; my bootsteps were muffled against the hardness.

"Okay." A hint of excitement quivered in Kara's voice. "You ready?"

"Sure." For what, I had no freaking idea.

Lexi pulled off my mask.

I gaped. *A photoshoot studio? What the . . . ?*

Carla, my band's makeup artist, rested her hip against the vanity station. Round light bulbs blazed brightly around the large mirror. Her makeup kit was sprawled across the table.

"Hey, gorgeous." Carla came over and gave me a hug.

"What's going on?" I glanced around the huge studio. Reflector shields, lights, fans, and a white backdrop were set up at the rear of the room. A pile of props—an assortment of sofas and loveseats, cabaret chairs, lamps, potted plants, and bar stools—filled the far corner. A rack of men's and women's clothes stood a few feet away.

"We wanted to do something special for you." A soft smile, full of tender warmth, spread across Kara's face. "We know it was a difficult decision for you to keep the baby and you haven't been yourself lately. So, we want to make you feel beautiful and amazing again. We've set up a photoshoot to help reignite your spark. We've prepared a day of dress-up fun."

Oh wow!

Lexi caught my hand in hers and gave it a gentle squeeze. "What you're doing is one of the most selfless things I've ever known. Having a baby when it's not what you originally planned blows my mind at how much you love Kyle. It's a massive, life-changing event and a huge commitment. Not to mention courageous."

Courageous? I felt anything but confident. Nausea was a constant presence in my stomach, and that wasn't just from morning sickness. It had been three days since I'd walked out of the clinic. The idea of having a baby still messed with my head. Would I ever find peace with the notion? Accept my decision?

When would my lingering anguish disappear? The jagged scars on my heart from my parents' lack of love were deep. But new fears beyond their abandonment and selfishness had risen. I worried I wouldn't be a good mom. I didn't know how to be one. The love Kyle and I shared would survive anything, but would we pass that love onto our baby? Would our child resent our career when music and performing often had to come first? Would they grow to hate or be jealous of our fame? Would our lifestyle cause our kid to become a recluse? How would Kyle and I make music and family work?

I swallowed the dry lump in my throat. "I question myself every second of the day on whether I've made the right choice. But then I see how happy Kyle is." I closed my eyes and pictured his smile and holding our baby in his arms. "I'm just focusing on that."

"Well, today we're focusing on you." Kara smiled at me as she took Ashleigh from Diego and gave her daughter a quick kiss on the cheek. Diego dug into his oversized baby bag and pulled out a playmat and some toys. He placed them on the floor by the side wall. Kara rocked Ashleigh on her hip. "Gem, it's time to bring back the goddess you are. Carla is going to spruce you up." Kara waved toward the rack of clothing. "I've got all these outfits for you to choose from. Lex is going to take your photos."

"Girls." Tears welled in my eyes. "This is incredible. But not necessary. I'm fine." I had eight months to get used to the idea of having a baby. *Ugh.* Plenty of time, right?

"Babe." Lexi swept my hair back over my shoulder. "You haven't been yourself. And that's okay. It's been a huge shock to the system. But you've made the call to have the baby, so it's time to own it. Accept that your body is gonna change, life is gonna change, and that there is no going back. You're strong. We want to remind you of that. I want to capture you during every stage of your pregnancy to show you how beautiful you are, inside and out, from now when you're not showing, to when you're about to burst that little McIntyre out of you."

I winced. "I really don't want to think about that part." Or my body never being the same.

"Gem." Kara rested her head against Ashleigh's. "You've inspired people all around the world with your music and ambition. Now you get to take that to the next level. Show people how incredible true love is, and how you can have it all. Career, love and family."

My heart threatened to fall onto the floor. The muscles in my jaw ached as I resisted the urge to cry. "I'm afraid—no, petrified—that this will ruin my career." Having a family was always different for women. Babies took up too much time. Impacted our bodies. Two of my rockstar friends had given up music to have children and showed no signs of returning to the stage. I didn't want that to happen to me. I didn't want to break my band's cycle of recording and touring. "How am I going to travel, write music, and perform with a kid in tow? And be a good mom?"

"You will need a Diego." Kara smiled at him. Diego held his hands out and clapped as he came over and took Ashleigh from Kara.

"Oh, Miss Gemma." Diego's eyes brightened as he tickled Ashleigh's tummy; she broke out in a gummy smile featuring two tiny bottom teeth. "I will look after your baby. And Lexi's when she has one, too. I love children."

"You're on." I didn't hesitate to take him up on his offer and slapped him on the shoulder.

"Yay!" Diego twirled Ashleigh around and headed over to the side of the studio to play with her.

"See?" Kara grabbed a black leather jacket off the rack and twinkled her fingers at Ashleigh. "It's all sorted. Diego Daycare is ready and waiting."

"And Gem, there's no chance of your career dying." Lexi nudged her elbow against my arm. "The guys won't let you contemplate that crap for one second. They're behind you one hundred percent. They love music just as much as you do." Lexi gave me an encouraging smile. "You can be a rockstar *and* a mom. Be the next Gwen, P!nk, Alicia, Madonna, Kelly, Christina, Adele—my God, there are so many women who still rock after having a family. I guarantee you'll be one of them." She sucked in a deep breath, and excitement flashed in her eyes. "While we're here doing a shoot to make you feel glamorous, the guys wanted to show you how much they support you too. So, to help light that fire under your butt, *they've* planned a gig for you tonight up in Midtown."

What? My heart stood to attention. Stage lights. Screaming fans. Music. *Incredible.* Tears prickled my eyes. "You've done all this for me?"

"Yes. But Kyle was behind most of it." Kara wrapped her arms around me and rocked me from side to side. "We jumped at the chance because we love you. He's been so worried about you and is beyond ecstatic that you've decided to have the baby." Kara stroked my hair. "Gem, you're gonna be an amazing mom. You're not alone. We're on this journey together. We will make changes and adjust. But I promise you this: we will enrich each other's lives, not hinder them. You hear me?"

"But Kar . . ." I closed my eyes. This was too much, too overwhelming. "We don't have time for a shoot. You and Hunt have a meeting with the surrogacy agency today." They were supposed to sign their new surrogacy agreement; she shouldn't be here.

"We changed our meeting to tomorrow." Kara's soft voice fluttered with kindness. "You're more important. Signing legal documents can wait another day."

"Come on." Lexi patted the back of the makeup chair. "It's time to shine. This will be good practice for the awards shows next month. Let Carla work her magic while I set up my gear."

"You girls . . ." I sank into the chair, amazed at how much my friends cared. It was nearly eleven o'clock, and my morning sickness hadn't subsided. But maybe a bit of pampering and showing off for a shoot was what I needed. Maybe this would help me feel like myself again.

Carla stood behind me and brushed my long hair.

Carla had been part of my team for seven years. Bec, our personal assistant, had been with us since the beginning. There were so many friendships that I held close to my heart. What would I do without these women? I'd probably miss flights, run late to shows, and stumble onto stage half-dressed.

Carla tossed the brush onto the table and grabbed her flat iron. She twisted a strand of my hair around the ceramic plates. "I'm gonna make you look super sexy. A badass supermom-to-be. Girl, you gonna be *hot.*"

I caught Carla's hand and gave it a gentle rub. "Thank you."

"Anything. Anytime, babe."

As Carla let a bouncing curl fall around my shoulders, I captured Kara's gaze in the mirror. "If I'm playing with the guys tonight, I'll have to get to sound check and help them set up our gear."

"Sweetie." Kara jammed her hand against her hip. "You are way past setting up your own equipment. We've got crew for that. The guys have arranged everything. Bec and Kate are posting on your social media accounts as we speak to promote the gig. Everything is under control. All you have to do is sit back and enjoy yourself."

"And Kyle did all this?" How had I not noticed something was going on? We were so in tune, held no secrets, and could almost read each other's thoughts. *Damn.* This baby nonsense had really messed with my head.

"Yes, he did." Lexi pulled off her lens cap and took a shot of me getting my hair done. "He's crazy about you."

Wow. "I need to call him. Thank him. Tell him . . ." I grabbed my cell phone from my purse. How could I put into words how he made me feel? How amazing he was? How much I loved him? He always knew just what I needed and put up with my crap. My heart fluttered against my ribs. *Holy crap. I'm performing tonight.* We hadn't rehearsed. "We need to sort out the set list for the show."

"Gem." Kara snatched my cell phone out of my hands. "Everything is sorted. The guys have taken care of everything."

Lexi clipped me over the back of the head. "So snap the fuck out of this doomsday gloomy bullshit, and let's have some fun." She dashed over to the side table laid out with food. Chester sat on a fold-out metal stool, nibbling on a sandwich. She waggled her finger at him. "Don't eat all the food."

"I won't." He licked his fingers. "But it is good."

Lexi giggled as she grabbed a bottle of champagne out of the bucket of ice. She waved the bottle toward Kara and me. "We have some non-alcoholic bubbles, some treats, and some tunes. So let's pump up the music"—she turned up the speaker—"eat, drink, and rock the hell out of this shoot."

Lexi's antics always made me laugh. My girlfriends were the best. They were so thoughtful, caring, and always here to kick my ass when needed.

Carla styled my hair, creating glossy, wavy curls that cascaded down the center of my back. She painted my face with glamorous makeup, highlighting my emerald eyes with gold glitter and coloring my lips in a deep red lipstick. Once she'd finished, Kara led me over to sift through the clothing. I slid my hand over shiny sequined dresses, soft leather pants, glittery tops, and sparkly outfits. I loved fashion. Designer clothes always made me feel like a million dollars. But I placed my hand on my belly. Was I showing? Would I fit into these tailored numbers?

"Pick anything you like." Kara draped a sheer, printed scarf around her neck and struck a pose. "It's all from Chanel, Dolce and Gabbana, Ivory Mink and Balenciaga."

I jutted my chin toward the nearby rack. "So why do you have men's gear here?"

"Just outfits." Kara fluttered her eyelashes. Her aloofness didn't go unnoticed. "I have to take them home for awards season."

Hmm. We had to play at the Global Music Awards, the Grammys, and the Brits, flying back and forth between London and LA like it was a drive across town over the next couple of weeks. But Kara's impish smile was impossible to ignore. What was she up to?

I pulled a black, long-sleeved, sparkly minidress off a hanger. I'd had enough surprises for one day, but it was best to just go with the flow. "Fine. Whatever. Let's do this."

Slipping into the gorgeous Chanel dress lifted my spirits. The second I stepped in front of the white backdrop, they jumped yet another notch. Kara turned the music up even louder, and Lexi clicked her camera. The electric vibe jumping around the room was contagious. I loved photo shoots. Making sexy eyes. A subtle lift of the shoulder. A smoldering pout. After years in the spotlight and a gazillion photographs, posing, playing up to the camera, and flirting with the lens came naturally to me.

With outfit change after outfit change, we laughed and messed around. Kara was in her element dressing me, and Lexi was in heaven behind the lens. Carla insisted on makeup touch-ups between takes.

But there was something missing. In the air. In my heart. In my soul.

My zing was only set to simmer, not at my usual revved rate.

Was it because the guys weren't here?

I rarely did shoots without them. We were a team, joined at the hip.

The heavy door to the studio swung open, and in strode the guys.

My heartbeat leaped toward the rafters. Hunter chuckled as he nudged a goofy-grinned Kyle inside. Hayden and security brought up the rear.

What the . . .? What are they doing here?

The three guys joined the girls at the edge of the backdrop draped over the floor. Sam and Mick joined Chester at the table of food and tucked into the treats.

"Gem?" Kara thrust her thumb toward Hunter and Kyle. "You are at your best with these two by your side. So let's get you firing on all cylinders and get them in front of the camera with you."

I cupped my hands over my mouth. My chest exploded with love. My friends knew me too well.

Kyle glided over to me and kissed my lips. "Hey, precious. How you doing?"

"Better now you're here," I whispered, rose on my tippy-toes, and wrapped my arms around his neck. "Thank you. But you didn't have to do this."

"I wish I could do something like this for you every day."

I cupped his cheek and pressed my lips against his mouth, so warm, tender, and full of sweetness.

"Okay, you two." Hunter clicked and snapped his fingers. "Let's get our groove on." He rubbed his hands together and headed toward the rack of clothing. He ripped a pair of leather pants off the hanger and tossed them at Kyle. "Get into these, bud."

Laughing, Kyle dragged me over to the outfits. Kara helped us coordinate leather pants and black tops.

Hayden leaned against the edge of the vanity mirror and folded his arms. "You guys do this way too often."

"What? Shoots?" Hunter ripped off his anorak and sweatshirt.

"Yeah." Hayden scratched the tip of his chin. "Don't you get sick of it? All the dressing up and posing and shit?"

"Never." Hunter buttoned up his slim-fitted black dress shirt that showed off his toned arms. "We were born to do this."

"Do you miss doing press since you left The Saylors?" I tugged on a pair of leather pants and zipped them up. Smoothing my hands over the soft fabric covering my thighs, my fingertips tingled. I loved the feel of leather against my skin.

"We never did many shoots. The cover of our single was a graphic, not a photo of us. And press? We didn't even do much of that when we had our one hit. So I don't know if I'm missing out because I've never really done it."

"Hayds, I photograph you all the time." Lexi pointed her lens at him.

His model-worthy smile lit his face. He was without a doubt a natural in front of the camera.

I giggled. "Whether you're in front of the camera or not, you'll get a huge following being our drummer."

"Nah." But his eyes brightened. His smile, a touch bashful. "I'm content to stay at the back of the stage."

Was he? Food for thought. But I had other things to focus on now.

Carla quickly styled Kyle's and Hunter's hair, then we were back in front of the camera.

Sitting between the two guys, on the floor with a black fluffy blanket draped around our waists and legs, we huddled in close. We posed, pulled faces, played it up for the camera—smiling, teasing, laughing—then we morphed our expressions into all-serious, seductive, come-fuck-me pouts.

Kyle nuzzled my neck and kissed beneath my earlobe. Goosebumps shot down my arm. "Hmm. You're so beautiful."

I lowered my eyelashes and blushed. "Thank you. Now focus."

"I am. On you."

Lexi darted around us, snapping away on her camera. "Lift your chin, Gem. Kyle, look here, not at Gem. Hunt, lean in closer. Work those sexy smiles for me. That's it."

Hunter chuckled and rested his head against mine. "How crazy is it we get to do this shit whenever we feel like it?"

"Yeah. It's pretty special." I glanced around the room at my friends. "We have an incredible life. But it's changing." Reality slammed into my chest and made it difficult to draw breath. "In ways I'd never anticipated."

Hunter nudged his elbow against my arm. "Yeah. But you've got this."

A wave of tears came over me, and I sniffled. *What the hell was that? Hormones? Fuck this shit.* "Thank you." I brushed my hand down his cheek. "I needed this."

"We know." Hunter kissed the top of my head. "You don't need shoots like this to prove how phenomenal you are. But I'm down for showing off anytime." His heartfelt tone warmed my heart, then a wicked grin curled across his lips. "But I can't wait to see you when you're covered in baby shit, have vomit in your hair, and look like hell after you haven't slept in days."

I punched him in the arm, hard. "I hate you."

"Ow! But I love you." His eyes glinted as he bumped his arm against mine. "You're brutal."

"You deserved it."

"Never," he joked as he scrambled to his feet. "I'll be back in a sec. I need to pee. When I return, we'll have to wrap up this shoot and get ready to play tonight. Yeah, baby." He gave me a high-five, pumped Kyle's fist, then dashed through the door on the side of the studio that led to the restrooms.

Kyle brushed his fingertip across my chin and turned my face toward him. "You better now?"

"Yeah."

His dark eyes drank me in like he needed my presence to breathe. My lungs ached because I felt the same way about him. He swung toward me and hooked his legs over mine, placing them on either side of my hips. He edged in close, threaded his hand beneath my hair, and massaged the base of my neck. "Gem, I'll do everything I can to make being pregnant as easy as possible for you. I'll do anything to help you through it. I know you're scared. So am I. But I know we're gonna love our baby. If it is loved even a fraction of how much we love each other, it's gonna be the most loved kid on the face of the planet."

I placed my hand on his heart. "I know. I just need more time to wrap my head around it."

"You have eight months."

"That all?" A smile tugged at the corner of my mouth.

"Yeah. That's all." He drew my lips to his and ignited them with a smoldering kiss. His fingertips caressed my neck, easing the tension from my muscles. Our hot breaths entwining heated my blood, quickened my pulse, and charged my heart.

"You know we're at a shoot, right?" I stole a glance toward our friends. Lexi was fiddling with her camera as she talked to Kara. Hayden was eating cake with Carla and our security team.

"Yep." He kissed my forehead, my cheek, and then my lips. "So I better stop before I can't or I don't want to."

I threaded and combed my fingers through his short hair. Was it possible to fall in love with him more than I already had? Was there a way to show him how much I loved him? *Oh yeah . . .* I was having his fucking baby.

"Oh. My. God." Lexi peered over her lens. "I just got some amazing shots. They're gorgeous."

"But we're on a break." Kyle groaned, half-heartedly.

"Nah." Lexi gave a carefree shrug of her shoulder. "Candid shots are often the best."

When Hunter returned, Lexi took more photographs of the three of us lying on the floor—from the front of us lazing together, and then from up above as we lay on our backs.

"That's a wrap." Lexi lowered her Canon DSLR, and walked over to her laptop to check the images she'd taken. "Guys, these shots are fabulous. We could use them for promo." But then she stopped scrolling and clicking. Her chin jerked back. Her eyes remained glued to her screen. Her eyebrows arched high. "But wow. This one is my favorite."

Kyle and Hunter helped me to my feet, and we gathered around the laptop. One of the first shots Lexi had taken filled the screen. I had on the stunning black mini dress. My arms were crossed over my chest. My chin was slightly raised. A fan had blown my long hair in soft waves around my head. My eyes were half closed, full of sexiness. My lips, slightly parted. A shot like this could grace the glossy pages of *Vogue*.

I blinked. Even I had to admit I looked hot.

"That . . . is *my* Gem." The possessive tone rumbling in Kyle's voice sent sparks to my core.

As he met my gaze, his eyes darkened. "You're so freaking gorgeous."

Heat flushed my cheeks. "You're not so bad yourself." I caught my bottom lip between my teeth and turned to take in my amazing friends. *Damn*. I loved these people. "Thank you for doing this. I feel better." But there was only one thing that never failed to get my spirit soaring, and that was music. In a few hours, I'd hit the stage with the guys. "I still have a long way to go to get my head around being pregnant, but I'm not backing down. You and music will see me through. So let's get the hell out of here and go rock up a storm."

"Hell yeah," everyone hollered and headed outside to the cars.

After an early dinner and a change into another gorgeous outfit of glittery jeans and a top that Kara had brought for me, security ushered us to the venue.

The moment I stood behind my mic, strummed my guitar and sang to the screaming crowd, I'd felt right at home, like myself.

I'd make a family and music work. There was no other option. My heart and soul wouldn't let me have it any other way.

I took a deep breath and sang.

> *I thought I was damaged goods, left shattered on the floor*
> *My heart was broken by the slam of a door*
> *Never thought it would beat like it did before*
> *I never thought that my love could ever be restored*
>
> *But I fell*
> *When you came to me*
> *Out of the blue*

Kyle threw me a heart-stopping grin as he stepped up to his mic. He flicked his hair off his forehead, pressed his lips against the mic, and sang.

> *You picked up the pieces, put me together again*
> *Your sweet kisses sent my head into a spin*
> *Your tender touch showed me what heaven meant*
> *If this is love, I'm ready to dive right back in*
>
> *I was gone*
> *When you came to me*
> *Out of the blue*

Hayden slammed out the raw, fast drumbeat behind us. The crowd's screams reached deafening heights when Hunter took to his mic to sing the chorus.

> *But before I give you my heart, please, promise me this . . .*

That you'll keep me grounded
Let my dreams grow unbounded
Keep my heart protected
Ensure this love never ends, oh yeah
'Cause baby, I wasn't prepared
No-oh-oh-oh
For you to come to me
Strike me down with love
Out of the blue

The song tapped into my soul. The guitar's vibrations reverberated through my veins. The lyrics struck me right in the center of my chest.

I'd been struck out of the blue with a baby. Every day, it grew inside me.

But when would the excitement come? When would my motherly instinct kick in? The urge to nurture fill my heart?

Fear gripped my throat. What if those things never came? What if I never connected with the baby? What if I regretted having a child for the rest of my life?

Fuck . . . no!

There'd be no regrets. I'd owned every damn decision I'd made in my life—the good and the bad. I'd learned from my mistakes and had sworn not to repeat any. I had to put my fears aside. There was time to bond with my baby. *Wasn't there?*

I hope so.

I was strong and determined. Kyle loved me. I had an amazing network of friends for support.

I'd survived in one of the toughest industries on the planet. Surely, I would do the same in parenthood.

Chapter 9

"Fuck. This. Shit." Shivering in the cold, I wrapped my arms around myself and jiggled on the spot. My breath misted. It must be less than zero degrees. Snow lined the sidewalk, blanketed the ground, and coated the trees in Central Park behind me. The city lights lit up Columbus Circle like a Christmas tree. Why couldn't I have met Hayden indoors, at the restaurant, or wherever the hell it was he wanted to take me? It was our third Valentine's Day together since we'd been married. But freezing off my tits and toes hadn't been on my agenda. *This* wasn't romantic.

I tugged my beanie lower to cover my ears, then tightened my scarf. I should've worn warmer clothes—not tights, a woolen dress, and a coat that barely covered my ass. After arriving home from the Grammys in LA yesterday—with Everhide carrying two new statues to add to their overflowing shelves of awards—I'd prefer to be at home, eating takeout and having my way with Hayden in bed, rather than going out. We'd been trying for a baby since Christmas, but I wasn't pregnant yet. And we'd been trying . . . a lot.

But Hayden had insisted on taking me out tonight.

Damn it. Where is he?

He'd told me he'd meet me here at six thirty. It was now six thirty-seven.

If he didn't hurry up, the people passing by might think I was the latest ice sculpture on display.

I glanced down the street toward the Plaza Hotel on the far corner. The way was lined with horses and carriages waiting for loved-up couples to take trips around the park. I wrinkled my nose. Nothing, not even the snow, could hide the stench of horse shit that hung in the air. I looked right, across the road toward the shopping center. Pedestrians dashed along the sidewalk. But there was no sign of Hayden.

I pulled out my cell phone and texted him.

ME: WHERE ARE YOU? IT'S FREEZING.

His reply was instant.

HAYDEN: ACROSS THE STREET.

What? Squinting into the evening darkness and peering into the buildings' shadows, I scanned the opposite sidewalk in each direction. All the men scurrying along looked the same dressed in dark coats with beanies jammed low on their heads, scarves tied around their necks and laptop bags slung over their shoulders.

Then, I spotted him.

My heart shook off the icicles and fluttered against my ribs.

Hayden's long ambling stride was impossible to miss. He held a huge bunch of red roses in one arm. His backpack was draped over his other shoulder. There wasn't a violent bone in my body, but I might commit murder for his long puffer jacket. He picked up his pace as he drew closer and dashed across the street.

He held out the flowers toward me. "Hi, Angel. Happy Valentine's Day."

"Thank you." I took the flowers and buried my nose in the blooms. The subtle hint of their sweet fragrance filled my senses. "They're beautiful. But I'm so cold." My voice shivered. "Where are we going?"

"I'll warm you up. Promise." Wrapping his arms around me, he drew my body flush against his. He dipped his head to kiss me, all sweet, hot, and spicy.

My knees weakened. He always kissed with a tease of his tongue. Just a subtle flick, a lick, a taste. Just enough to send sparks of electricity jolting between my legs.

"That better?" He grinned, running his gloved fingertips down my jawline.

"Yeah." His kiss had definitely warmed my cheeks.

"Shall we?" He held out his crooked arm.

"As long as we're going somewhere warm."

"I hope we are."

I curled my arm around his elbow, and he led me along the park's fence line toward Fifth Avenue. "Sorry I'm late. I got held up at the store. I greatly underestimated the rush of people buying last-minute Valentine's gifts. But I had to get you some flowers." At the first horse carriage, he halted and waved me toward the massive white cart. "Shall we?"

"We're going on a carriage ride?" My teeth chattered. "In this weather?"

"Yep. It'll be fun."

The temperature was dropping. I hoped he was right. "Okay."

The driver met us at the carriage door. "Good evening. I'm Dimitris." His broad Russian accent clipped through the cold as he dipped his head and touched the rim of his fluffy trapper hat with earflaps. "I'll be your driver tonight."

My fingers twitched inside my woolen coat pockets. I'd never stolen anything in my life, but the driver's headgear looked mighty tempting, toasty, and warm. *Stupid cold has messed with my brain.*

Dimitris opened the door and pulled down the carriage step. "Please, hop on board." He held out his hand to help me into the cart. Hayden climbed in behind me.

We sat on the red velvet seat, and the driver grabbed blankets out of the wooden box at the front of the carriage. "There are plenty of blankets. Rug up. Snuggle up. And enjoy the romantic ride through the park on this magical Valentine's evening."

I wasn't so sure it was magical. But I was more frozen than

Elsa.

Dimitris clambered into the driver's seat, took the reins, and steered the huge black horse through the gates into Central Park.

The horse's hooves clopped against the wet road. The carriage's wheels squelched through puddles of water. I giggled and shivered as I snuggled into Hayden. The warmth from his body and the blankets slowly defrosted my insides. "This is sweet." I didn't want to hurt his feelings; he'd been so excited about today. "But ridiculous in this weather."

"We're always down for doing crazy shit." Hayden nudged my arm. His dark eyes glinted in the soft light. "How about some champagne?" He dug into his bag and drew out a bottle. "We have to celebrate Valentine's Day."

I'd rather have a steaming hot chocolate, but I loved champagne. I snapped on a smile and rubbed my gloved hands together. "Sure. Alcohol better warm me up."

"I wasn't expecting it to be this cold." His breath misted as he popped open the Bollinger and poured it into two plastic flutes. "It's only slightly cooler out here than in our apartment when the heating fails."

My gaze narrowed as I took my drink. There it was. The sly dig. Hayden had subtly dropped more and more hints about moving since Christmas. But we couldn't afford a place closer to our friends. I adored our cozy, rundown, *in-desperate-need-of-renovations, full-of-memories* apartment. We'd put a hole in the wall near the kitchen when we'd dropped a box while moving in. Hayden's drum kit had scratched the floorboards in the living room. I'd stained the bathroom tiles from developing negatives and drying photographs. And we'd broken the shower curtain rail while having sex and had stuck it back together with duct tape. So many memories. I never wanted to leave. "Our *home* is *never* this cold. Not ever."

But somewhere more modern with more room and better heating would be nice. *Ugh.* He'd messed with my head. *Damn you, Hayds.*

After storing the bottle, he edged closer to me and drew the two fluffy blankets up to our chests. He clinked his plastic flute against mine. "To my Angel. Happy Valentine's Day. And may we have many, many more."

My jaw ached in the chilly air. "Uh-huh. Cheers."

As we sipped our drinks, the cart lurched along the lamp-lit road through the gardens. The slight breeze brushed against my face, and my teeth chattered. I had to get out of this weather soon or I'd end up as frozen as the pond.

Hayden wrapped his arm around my shoulders and burst out laughing. "Shit, it's cold. I really didn't think this through, did I? I wanted this to be romantic, but I'm freezing my balls off."

"My tits fell off back at the park's entrance. I'm aching all over."

"Me too. Luckily, it's only a short ride." He downed his drink, then wrinkled his nose and waved his empty flute toward the front of the cart. "And do all horses smell this bad?"

"I'm not sure it's the horse." I tilted my chin toward the driver.

Hayden chuckled, drew me closer, and kissed me.

Mmm. His lips always tasted like warm, delicious honey.

He hooked one of my stray curls behind my ear. "Hopefully our next destination will be better. I don't want this to turn into the Valentine's date from hell."

If it did, and we could laugh about it, it wouldn't matter. "As long as there is heating and I'm with you, it'll be fine."

After our fifteen-minute *not-so-romantic* ride around the park, Hayden took my hand and we scurried down Eighth Avenue. "I got a reservation at this place Adam always raves about. He said the burgers are wicked."

I had my doubts. Adam, Everhide's backup band guitarist, partied harder than all my friends put together. A true jokester, he was often high when not on tour and probably didn't know where he was or what he was eating half the time. But he was a cool friend and a freakishly talented musician.

Hayden led me up a few narrow concrete steps to the hole-in-the-wall industrial-urban-styled café restaurant. "This place better be good."

He opened the door. The bell chimed, and we stepped inside.

The glossy dark wooden bar toward the back of the venue glistened in the soft lighting. Couples filled the tiny tables that were crammed along the brick wall and in the area by the front window. The copper pots that hung from wrought-iron hooks above the wood-fired oven looked like they were for decorative purposes only and had never been used.

But the warmth hit me like a gentle, rolling wave. *Finally. Some heat.*

As I slipped off my coat and scarf, I wriggled my aching toes and my insides slowly melted like marshmallows over a campfire. I licked my lips, and my tummy grumbled. "Babe, you had me at burgers." I'd love a loaded meat sandwich with gooey cheese, crispy bacon, and caramelized onion. With a side of fries.

But the smell coming from the kitchen wasn't quite right. *What is that? Mushrooms?*

A short, bubbly girl who looked like she was of high school age finished typing an order at a nearby table into her tablet, then headed over to greet us. "Hi. Welcome to EarthRuby Café. Happy Valentine's Day. Do you have a reservation?"

"Yes." Hayden nodded. "It's under 'Moore.'"

The girl scanned the booking list on the counter and ticked off our name. "Excellent." She picked up two menus, threw Hayden a saucy smile and totally ignored me. "I'm Fleur. I'll be your server this evening. Let me show you to your table. This way, please."

We followed her halfway down the café. The brick walls amplified the noise from the open kitchen and restaurant full of guests. But as we took our seats, Fleur eye-fucked Hayden while she poured us glasses of water. There was nothing subtle about her checking him out. I couldn't blame her. Hayden was hotter than Ryan Reynolds and Ryan Gosling combined.

Back off, bitch. He's mine.

"The specials are on the board above the bar." Fleur waved toward the blackboard covered in yellow cursive writing. She leaned forward, giving Hayden an eyeful of the decent cleavage bulging out of her low-cut T-shirt. "I highly recommend the pumpkin soup appetizer. It's rich. Creamy. And totally delicious."

My eyebrows shot skyward. *My God!* Did this girl just want to slide onto Hayden's lap and go for it?

Hayden shook his head and threw me an *I'm-sorry* wince. He lifted his gaze to Fleur. "Thank you. But we'll order drinks first." He reached across the table and entwined his fingers with mine. "I'll have a Budweiser, and my gorgeous *wife* will have a vodka, lime, and soda."

"Oh . . . right." Fleur's shoulders deflated but she snapped on a fake smile, regaining a sliver of professionalism. "Yes . . . of course." She tapped the order into her tablet. "I'll give you a few minutes to peruse the menu. I'll be back to take your order shortly." Fleur spun on her heels and headed toward the bar.

I burst out laughing. "Oh, babe. You just broke her heart." Seriously? What was Fleur thinking? That she'd hook up on Valentine's Day?

"Sometimes, you have to be cruel to be kind." Hayden sighed, leaned forward, and lowered his voice. "But what else could I do? I already belong to somebody." He ran his thumb over the tattoo of his name on my wrist. *Too sweet.*

"So true." I tugged my hand free and picked up the menu. "But can we order? I'm starving." *Yep.* I'd burned a gazillion calories trying to keep warm in the snow. I needed to refuel my system. But as I skimmed the menu, I furrowed my brow. I pursed my lips and glanced at Hayden. "Hayds . . . um . . ."

"Oh, shit." He scanned the list. The color drained from his face. "There's no fucking meat in these burgers. It's all vegetarian. Vegan. What the fuck?"

"It's okay." I half-giggled, half-cried. My stomach groaned in protest. "I'm sure there is something we can eat." After reviewing restaurants for years, I should've been more aware of the style of food they served when I'd walked past the picture of mushrooms on the wall.

"Nothing against vegans, but we fucking love meat. I want cow. I want a big, juicy, steak burger." Hayden rubbed his brow. "This really has turned into the worst Valentine's ever." He slumped in his chair. "I'm sorry. I wanted everything to be perfect. But the weather is awful. The horse smelled bad. I made a reservation at a vegan restaurant. The waitress shoved her tits in my face. Your flowers have seen better days." The poor things hadn't handled the dash along the street well; now, they wilted in the warmth on the table. "It's crap."

I giggled and reached for his hand. "Hayds, it's fine. Why don't we just order something quick, pick up a pizza from Joe's on the way home, and then cuddle up in front of the TV and watch a movie?"

"But we do that all the time."

"I've never been one to celebrate Valentine's Day. Neither have you."

"But—"

"Excuse me?" The brunette at the table next to ours leaned across the aisle. Her voice was meek and jittery. "Are you Hayden Moore? Everhide's drummer?"

Hayden's cheeks darkened by ten shades of red. "Yeah."

Her hands shot over her mouth, then fell to her chest. "Oh my God." She shrieked loud enough for the whole restaurant to hear. Heads turned. "I'm such a huge fan. You're amazing. I went to your show at The Garden. Wow. You are so much better-looking in real life, I mean, close up, I mean . . . Oh shit. I'm rambling."

Her boyfriend mouthed, *"I'm sorry."*

More guests' eyes widened as they recognized Hayden.

I leaned forward and whispered to him, "I always told you one day you'd be famous."

Working for one of the biggest bands in the world had slowly erased Hayden's anonymity. He should've considered that his growing popularity might have caused issues when we headed out. But it was pretty cool being noticed. It was still new and sent a buzz skipping across my skin. My heart swelled to the size of the moon. I was so proud of him. He'd worked hard and had finally gotten the break he deserved.

But this was our night. Private time.

So much for spending a romantic evening together.

"Can I get a photo?" The girl's voice was pitched as high as an excited teenager's.

Hayden's gaze flicked to me. A flurry of *oh-my-God-I've-just-been-recognized* excitement, and *shit-I've-screwed-up-our-evening* disappointment swirled in his eyes.

It was the first time a fan had spotted him without our friends around. I wouldn't take this moment away from him. We might get sick of the attention eventually, but right now . . . *It was freaking awesome!* I dipped my chin and waved my hand. "Sure. Go for it."

But after one photo, another four guests from nearby tables asked Hayden for pictures. So did the flirty server and the dreadlocked chef, who offered us a complimentary appetizer of Turkish bread and dips as a thank you. *Score!*

As Hayden humbly soaked up the attention, I snapped the shots. Everyone wanted a piece of my man—a photo, an autograph, a chance to say hello. *So cool.*

Once the commotion had calmed down, Hayden slumped in his chair. "I'm so sorry. I didn't think about the fans. I should've booked a more discreet restaurant. I'm still getting used to this whole celebrity thing."

"You big stud. My rockstar." I dunked a piece of bread into the beetroot dip and then took a nibble. "At least I'm the one who gets to take you home."

We were still adjusting to being part of the Everhide family. More recognition. More travel. Longer hours at work. But it was where we belonged. We were doing what we loved. Our dreams had come true.

He leaned forward and lowered his voice. A mischievous smile curled at the corners of his mouth. "Wanna do that now?"

"Yes, please."

"Let's get out of here."

After finishing our drinks, we headed home. We picked up a loaded meatlovers' pizza from Joe's on the way.

Sitting beside each other on the floor in our tiny apartment, we laughed about our crazy evening. The aroma of roasted garlic, cheese, and pepperoni filled the air. "Yum. Now this is decadence." I giggled as mozzarella cheese stretched from my mouth to my half-eaten pizza slice.

"Joe's does a wicked meatlovers'." Hayden grabbed another helping. "I'm sorry our Valentine's evening didn't turn out as planned."

"What?" I covered my mouth with my hand and shook my head. "In a warped way, it was fun. We'll look back on this day and laugh about it when we tell our kids."

"Yeah?" He dropped his crust into the pizza box and swiveled to face me. He arched an eyebrow. His dark eyes glinted with pure sexiness. "Did you say *kids*? Do you mean there will be more than one?"

I wiped the corner of my mouth with my fingertips, then licked the cheesy grease off my thumb and index finger. "We have to have at least two."

He ran his hand around my thigh. The warmth of his touch penetrated through my tights and meandered across my flesh. "Lex, we can't fit two kids in this place. *We* barely fit. One baby will be a struggle. We need a bigger place."

"They'll fit." I flicked my hand toward my old bedroom. "We'll buy twin beds. It'll be fine. Tiny house living is on trend. We'll just be doing it in a small apartment in the middle of Manhattan."

He took my hand in his. "Angel, if we're going to have a family, we have to move. I've talked to the bank. We can't afford much. But if we can find an older apartment, one that needs renovations, we'll fix it up over time. We'll make it our own."

"Why do you want to move?"

"I want to create new memories in our own place. I don't want to pay rent for the rest of our lives."

He had a point, but we'd only been on decent incomes since

joining Everhide three years ago. Even so, we weren't on big bucks. We were employees. "Can we not worry about this now?" I grabbed another slice of pizza, then stared at the greasy topping. My heart took a plunge to the bottom of the ocean. I lowered my chin. "We haven't even got one baby. One is not even on the way."

He kissed the tip of my shoulder. "It will happen."

"How? When?" Frustration edged into my tone. I picked a piece of pepperoni off my slice, popped it in my mouth, and chewed. "Now we've decided to have a baby, it's not happening." I prayed I wouldn't have trouble getting pregnant.

"I'm happy to make love whenever you want too." His gaze turned from warm to smoldering hot. He grabbed my slice of pizza and placed it back in the box. "How about now?"

My pulse skipped back to life. He scrambled to his feet, took my hand, and dragged me to stand. Before I had time to blink, he steered me backward toward our bedroom and onto the bed. Crawling over me, he edged between my legs and lowered his weight onto me. He smoothed his hands over my curly hair. "I love you. Wanna make a baby?"

My heart happy danced around the room. "Yeah."

Clothes were speedily discarded into a pile on the floor. Our naked bodies were quick to connect. My eyes fluttered closed. Hayden's kisses stole my breath. Every sensual brush of his lips and spicy flick of his tongue quickened my heartbeat. Our love-making was hot enough to melt my bones. I needed that after nearly freezing to death earlier in the evening.

Lying in a tangle of limbs and arms in the aftermath of a wicked orgasm, I placed my hand on my abdomen.

"Lex?" Hayden straightened the quilt over our naked bodies. "You okay?"

"Yeah. Totally." I smiled as I ran my palm over my lower belly. "It's weird. But . . . I feel different. I don't know how to describe it. It's ridiculous, right? But I think we just made a baby?"

"You can't tell that quickly just by a feeling." Grooves furrowed deep into his brow. "Can you?"

"I don't know. But let's hope so."

Maybe this Valentine's Day would turn out better than planned after all.

***

Two weeks later, I took a home pregnancy test. My hands shook as I placed the stick on the bathroom sink to process.

While waiting for the result, I paced the length of our tiny living room. Hayden sat on the edge of the sofa, twirling his drumsticks around in his hands. I stared at the timer on my cell phone. The test only took two minutes, but it seemed to take forever. Each second seemed to take ten times longer than usual.

The alarm sounded.

I glanced at Hayden. He stilled his sticks, placed them on the sofa, then jumped to his feet. I placed my shaky hand on his chest. His heart thundered as fast as mine. "You ready?"

He swept his hand through his hair. "Uh-huh. I think so."

We rushed into the bathroom and peered at the test stick resting on top of the box. The word 'Pregnant' filled the digital display.

"Oh, shit." Shock shot through Hayden's voice. "We did it."

"Ahhhh!" I shrieked, jumped up and down, then flung my arms around his neck. "We're pregnant."

Hayden picked me up and twirled me around. "This is incredible. I told you it would happen."

"Oh my goodness." I trembled all over. "This is amazing. We're gonna have a baby."

He caressed my face and kissed me.

The flick of his tongue ignited a new fire in my heart, one that blazed for the little baby that grew inside me.

"God, I love you." Hayden smiled against my lips.

A tear escaped and slid down my cheek. "And I love you."

We may have conceived at some other point in time before or after Valentine's Day, but nothing would change my mind. I was convinced it had happened that night.

I glanced around our bathroom and out across our apartment. I didn't know how we'd fit a family in here, but we would. I didn't want to move. Somehow, we'd make the small space work.

This was home. This was where my family belonged.

Chapter 10

GEMMA

I flicked a *hi, don't-let-me-disturb-you* wave to Hunter sitting in his office, talking on his cell phone, then headed down the hallway to his home studio. I itched to start our new album. But the butterflies in my stomach weren't just for music. A crazy idea had brewed in the back of my mind. I had to talk to Kyle and Hunter before Hayden joined us in an hour.

Taking a seat at the digital piano, I wiped my hands across my abdomen. *Shit!* My focus on music evaporated. I pulled my Pink Floyd T-shirt—one I'd stolen from Kyle—over the tiny bulge in my belly and puffed air through my nose. I was barely showing at three and a half months pregnant but wanted to keep my bump hidden. Denial and travel had helped the past few weeks disappear. But soon, Kyle's T-shirts and my sweatpants would be the only things that fit. Gone were my days of wearing tight jeans, tiny T-shirts, short skirts, and cut-off shorts. They were my thing—not oversized, frumpy maternity wear.

I wriggled on the stool, sat straight, and played. A tune of turmoil drove my fingers across the keys. Being pregnant was still surreal. Kyle fussed over me. He was beyond loving and adoring. The happiness that radiated off him bewildered me. But I still waited for that *oh-wow-I'm-pregnant* buzz to hit my heart.

I still felt . . . nothing. Other than anxious. Other than ill. Morning sickness lingered all day like the dull static in a short-circuiting speaker.

Why wasn't I normal?

Why couldn't I be thrilled?

When would the queasiness disappear?

But today wasn't about babies; it was about new music. And after today, maybe the guys and I would head in a new direction.

The studio door swung open. Hunter rushed in. I didn't even flinch. I was so used to him charging into rooms—it had no impact anymore. But the electric energy bursting off him filled the room and sparked my skin. His azure eyes were as lit as the Las Vegas Strip. He raced over to me and dragged me to my feet. He wrapped his arms around my waist, picked me up, and swung me around.

"What the hell?" I laughed as he put me on my feet.

"Where's Kyle?" He glanced toward the drums, the sofa, and then the desk.

"Haircut. He'll be here soon."

Hunter bent his knees, met me eye to eye, and splayed his hands by my face. His grin was as wide as the Milky Way.

My God? Was he going to launch through the roof? Do a Tom Cruise on the sofa?

"Nae's pregnant," he hollered, catching my shoulders and giving me a gentle shake. "That was Kar on the phone. She's at Nae's with Ashleigh. Nae's only had the embryo implanted for three weeks. But she hasn't lost the baby. It's ridiculously way too early to be this excited, but if successful . . . we'll have another kid in early December."

December? My blood pressure soared and my heart crashed onto the floor. *Shit!* We'd postponed the release of our new album once already because of my due date. But now, with Hayden and Lexi expecting, and Hunter and Kara having another child, it blew our agenda out to next year. Being aware of the possibility that my friends could have children, didn't make the reality of it sit any easier in my stomach. This meeting had gotten worse before it had even begun. *Too many babies.*

"Shit," I mumbled but was quick to drum up a cheery smile. "I mean, congratulations. I'm so happy for you. But . . . that's when we'd planned to launch our album."

I wanted to have my baby in September and be in full swing, promoting our new music, within three months. We'd churned out back-to-back albums and tours since we'd finished high school. Now that we had creative control and had proven ourselves as artists out from underneath the hit-making machine of SureHaven Records, we'd agreed to ease off the throttle and not put ourselves under so much pressure to make the next album. But the date of the next release kept blowing out. It was time to write and record. Another baby due would alter the schedule again.

Fuck.

Why did babies have to throw our plans into turmoil?

"Yeah, pushing out the release again sucks hairy balls." He rubbed my arms. "But it'll be okay."

I clenched my teeth and tensed my hands. "No. It won't."

Hunter's elation washed from his face like a tsunami wiped out an island. In its place, heartfelt concern darkened his eyes. "Gem? It will be. Trust me." He reached for my hand and jerked his head toward the sofa. "Come sit for a sec."

"No. I'm fine."

Of course, he ignored me. I twisted my wrist to pull my hand free, but his grip was like a vise. He tugged me across the room to the sofa and ordered me to sit.

"I can tell you're not." He fell onto the seat beside me. As he swiveled to face me, his knee butted mine. He lowered his voice. "We don't talk as much as we used to. I miss that." He took my hand and held it against his thigh. "But don't lie to me. We're past that, remember? Kyle isn't here. So talk. What's up? Is this about babies or music?"

I closed my eyes, searching my soul for an answer. Grit set in my bones. "I need music to keep me occupied. To give me something to focus on. I try *not* to think about the baby. I don't want to think about it."

But who was I kidding? It consumed nearly every thought. I'd struggled through award ceremonies and our performances over the past few weeks with severe nausea. New aches and pains had invaded my body. I refused to talk about being pregnant in interviews, determined to keep my personal life separate from our music, like we'd always done. But before my life changed forever, I wanted another album recorded and ready to release. I didn't want to have the finished product sitting there doing nothing for months.

Hunter waggled a finger toward my stomach. "You're getting to the point where you can't avoid this."

"Yeah." I leaned back against the sofa and brushed my hands over my barely there bump. "I'm suffering already. On top of all-day morning sickness, my boobs hurt all the time. I need to pee every hour, on the hour. I'm getting fat. No one will want to see this on stage." I circled my hands over my belly like it was the size of a basketball. "I'm afraid I will never go back to normal."

"Geez." Hunter half-smirked and chuckled. "And I thought I was the vain one?"

I lowered my chin and pinched my eyebrows together. "I just need music to distract me from all the shit my body is going through."

He rubbed and patted my knee. "I know you do. But stop worrying. I promise, we're never gonna stop making music. We're just gonna slow down for a while. We'll adjust. Having this baby is gonna be life-changing, but it's not a lobotomy. I swear."

"I'm sure someone has given me one." I grabbed the cushion from behind me and hugged it against my chest. "I can't get my head around how Kyle and I will make this work. It's different for you and Kar. When you're on stage, she's not. Same with Hayds and Lex. Even with Diego onboard, how can Kyle and I do this when we're at rehearsals, writing, recording, or performing at the same time? When we're doing back-to-back eighteen-hour days, promoting and touring? I don't want our kid to grow up feeling rejected and unloved or constantly left in the care of a nanny. Or even worse, left at home alone when they were older." *Oh my God.* Just like my mother had done to me. "I'm afraid I'm just like my mom." *Selfish, self-centered bitch.*

Was that why I hadn't connected with the baby?

I *was* just like my mother?

Fuck!

"No, Gem. Never." He shook his head and tucked his hair behind his ear. "Your heart is full of love and devotion. Your baby will be surrounded by people who love them. We have Nanny Diego. Our troop of kids will be with us all the time. We're gonna take them on the road. They'll go to school together or be home tutored. Who knows? Who cares? That's five years away. Having a kid changed Kara, so if that can happen, anything is possible."

True. Kara no longer obsessed about spending every second of the day with Ashleigh or worried about enrolling her in private schools, kindergarten, and extracurricular activities. That had been a brain-altering change, but it was for the better. She was thriving as our stylist, designing and being a mom.

He leaned back against the sofa. With our shoulders touching, he angled his head toward me. "We'll get through this together. Kyle and I aren't going anywhere. We will make music and perform until the day we die. We will rock the shit out of this parenting thing. You grow into a more powerful, inspiring, incredible woman every day . . . Okay, she might have gone AWOL for a bit, but she's back. You think you won't love your child, but I know you will. You're the one who brought us together—You, me and Kyle in high school; Lexi when we first moved to Manhattan; Hayden from the first party we threw at our old apartment; and then Kara from our first fitting at Conrad's; not to mention everyone in our fab management team. That is why you're gonna be an incredible mom and love your baby. I guarantee it. Because you're all about family."

"I'm scared of screwing up."

"So am I. We can fuck up our kids' lives together."

"Promise?"

"Always." He hooked his arm around my shoulders and kissed the top of my head. "Guess you don't want to hear that you're glowing?"

I punched him in the arm, hard. "No. I don't."

"Ow!" He fell sideways against the padded arm of the sofa and held up his hands. "Wait. It's true." He sweetened his tone and circled his hand in front of my face. "You look kinda adorable pregnant, all rosy-cheeked." The corner of his mouth curled into a devilish smile. "Your boobs are *definitely* bigger. You're even more stunning, sexy, and beautiful than ever before. Super-cute."

My hands curled into fists. *Cute? I'm not fucking cute.* "I'm gonna kill you." I stood, knelt on the sofa, and hammered him with play-punches and tickles.

"Hey!" Kyle walked into the studio, carrying a takeaway bag of food in one hand and a pack of four bottles of water tucked under his other arm. "Shit. What did you do, Hunt?" He dropped the bag and waters onto the coffee table. "Why is Gem upset?" He dashed around the table to my side. "Babe, you okay?"

"Hunt said I looked cute pregnant." I sneered at Hunter. He just laughed.

"Well . . . he's right." Kyle smiled, bent down, and kissed my lips. "You look radiant."

Radiant? Who wants to be cute and radiant? I sneered at him too, then flopped onto the sofa. "Yeah . . . well . . . I'm not feeling it. Especially when the smell of whatever you bought is making me want to throw up."

"Oh, crap." Kyle winced. "I bought wraps."

"Gem? You've turned into a pussy." Hunter laughed. Grabbing a cushion, he held it up like a shield and jumped out of my reach before I could punch him again. He took to the floor and sat next to the coffee table. After ripping into the bag of food, he tossed me the packet of dry crackers. "Guess these are for you?"

"Yep." They were the only things I could stomach most days. "You should try being pregnant sometime."

"Nope. I'm good." Hunter handed out the waters, then jutted his chin toward Kyle. "Nice haircut. You trying to look like a Hemsworth?"

He chuckled as he rubbed his new short 'do. "Dude, they copy me. Not the other way around."

"Doesn't matter." Hunter shrugged his shoulder, then tore open his wrap. "I'll still win 'Sexiest Man Alive.'"

"You're so full of yourself." I giggled as I nibbled on a cracker. Hanging out and goofing around with these guys always made me feel better. "Who needs a Hemsworth, anyway?" I turned to Kyle and kissed his cheek. "Babe, you're way sexier. And hotter. And *soooo* much more handsome. Totally cute."

"You're right." Smiling, he shook his head. "Being called cute sucks. We're not fifteen anymore." He swiped his lunch off the table. "So? Why were you beating up Hunt when I walked in?" He opened his wrap and held it near his mouth, ready to take a bite. "Was there a reason other than him calling you cute?"

"Gem's concerned about the album." Hunter took a swig of water, then licked his lips. "We may have to delay the release again. Nae's three weeks pregnant."

"Holy fuck." Kyle high-fived Hunter across the table. "Congrats, man. That is awesome." Kyle swallowed his mouthful of chicken and twisted toward me. "Pushing back the album for another couple of months will be okay. In fact, it will be awesome. We'll get to spend more time with our baby before we hit promo."

Hunter covered his lips with his hand and spoke with his mouth half-full. "Nae is due the second week of December, then it's Christmas, and Kar will be busy until after Fashion Week in Feb. I can't see us hitting promo before March."

A cracker snapped in my hand. *Fuck.* March? That was a whole year away. "But we'll have Diego."

"Gem." Hunter puffed air through his nose and shook his head. "You have no idea what you're in for. A newborn is exhausting. Even that timeframe may get pushed back."

"What? No."

"Hey?" Kyle nudged his elbow against my arm. "It's okay. We have to be flexible. We're all itching to release new music." He glanced from me to Hunter, then back again. He licked his lips and swallowed hard. "But maybe writing a whole new album is out of the question for now."

"What?" Hunter and I shrieked in unison.

"Wait." He held up his hand. "Hear me out. I have a solution. Why don't we just release a couple of singles this year? We have a ton of tracks we could choose from and refine or write something fresh."

I sat four inches taller. My head stopped wheeling.

Singles would work.

Absolutely. Yes!

Kyle counted out his points on one hand. "We could release a track in late May, then one in mid-August before Gem's due and possibly one in January if we're up for it. All could be done with minimal promo. This gives us room to be flexible around the kids. If we hold off writing the album until next year, we'll be more in tune with the direction we want to take our music in and be more prepared to hit promo and tour."

He was right. My heart restarted. Blood re-entered my veins. Releasing singles would give me music to focus on. And take my brain off babies. *Brilliant!*

My skin prickled with renewed excitement. The notion that had been brewing inside my head jumped to the forefront of my mind. My pulse quickened as I curled my shaking hand around Kyle's thigh, and I smiled across at Hunter. I took a deep breath. The embers in my stomach glowed brightly, ready to ignite. "I love the idea of singles, but there is something else we need to discuss. It's about Hayden."

Kyle grimaced, grabbed a bottle of water, and twisted off the cap. "What about him?"

As we ate our lunch, I divulged my plan. The guys' mouths gaped at first, but then, we fell into deep discussion, weighing up the pros and cons, the for and against. No element went untouched.

This impacted our future. It was more explosive than an asteroid hitting the Earth. This would alter our center of gravity. But at the end of our conversation, my heart swelled with hope.

"So, what do you think?" I asked.

"Fuck." Shock scraped through Hunter's husky voice. "This is a massive change."

"But are you okay with it?" I drew a deep breath. "Do you need more time to think it over?" I'd lock the idea away for another time if they weren't ready to go down this path or let it go entirely if they never wanted to head in this direction. We didn't do anything in our band without all three of us being on board one hundred percent. I nudged my knee against Kyle's thigh. "What about you, babe?"

He blinked the wild bewilderment from his eyes and scratched his soft stubble. "Yeah." His breath rushed from his lungs. "It's huge. But the timing is right."

Hunter's brow furrowed as he stared at a spot on the rug. His concern morphed into a smile that filled my chest with warmth. "I'm in." He shook his head and chuckled. "Gem, being pregnant has definitely screwed with your head. But this change is brilliant."

There was a knock at the door.

It opened, and in walked Hayden.

Perfect timing.

He halted in the doorway, his hand still on the door handle. His gaze darted between us. "Guys? What's going on?"

Hunter pointed to the floor beside him. "Take a seat, bro. We have to talk."

"O-kay." Hayden hesitated before pulling his drumsticks out of his back jeans pocket and fell onto the rug beside Hunter. "S'up?"

I summoned my best poker face, but my insides jumped around on pogo sticks. Containing excitement wasn't my forte. "It's about the album."

Kyle clutched my hand, entwined our fingers, and then held them against his leg. "Hayds, with all the babies we're producing over the next several months, we're not going to rush into writing another album. With Gem due in September, Lexster in early November, and now Nae hopefully in December, we won't hit the studio hard until this time next year."

"Shit." Hayden's shoulders slumped. "So what does that mean? I don't have work until then?" But he quickly sat upright, shook his head, and spun toward Hunter. "Oh crap. Sorry, man. Is Nae pregnant?"

"Yeah."

"That's fucking awesome." He slapped Hunter on the shoulder.

Hunter grinned, took a sip of water, then wiped his mouth on the back of his hand. "It is. But this doesn't mean you get to slack off. It's the opposite, actually. We'll write and release a couple of singles this year instead of doing a full album. We want to start on them now."

"Oh." Hayden grabbed one of his sticks and tapped it between his palm and his thigh. *Tap-tap-tap-tap-tap.* "So, you don't need me today?"

Disappointment hovered low in his tone. He'd never written with us before. He'd only been involved in the final production of our songs.

But I hoped that was about to change.

I clutched Kyle's hand tighter to keep myself steady. My heart hammered against my ribs. "Hayds, we loved working with you on the last album. You're wickedly creative and super talented. So . . . we've talked and were wondering if you want to step up your game. We want to work with you from scratch on our new songs—lyrics, music, and the full production. But in addition to that . . . we'd officially like you to stand beside us . . . as one of us. As Everhide. What do you say?"

His eyes widened; the whites of his eyes were as bright as a full moon. "But . . . but the three of you are Everhide. I'm just your drummer."

"You're so much more than that." Kyle splayed a hand over his heart. "You're our best friend. You're one of us. You're Everhide too."

"But I don't want to stop drumming. My singing isn't that great. I don't want to prance around the front of the stage beside you."

"That's not what we meant." Hunter chuckled. "We want you to be a permanent fixture and to be part of every step of the process."

"Holy shit!" Hayden laughed but his eyes watered. He rubbed his drumstick up and down his thigh. "I'm ... I'm beyond stoked."

"It's time for a change." Kyle nodded slowly. "We've changed. Anything and everything we do from now on, we want you by our sides at events and shows, during writing and recording, making film clips, and doing interviews and photo shoots. You're always with us, so why not be part of all the fun?"

"But what about the other guys in the backup band? Adam? Joey? Link? They've played for you longer than I have."

I cuddled in closer to Kyle's side and rested my head against his shoulder. Hayden was like me—he always looked out for our friends. "Hayds, those guys are awesome. They work on other projects and tour with other artists. They're lifelong friends, absolutely. We love them to pieces. But if you come on board, and we venture in a new direction, we may not use a backup band in the future. It might just be the four of us. Those guys aren't family like you are."

"You think that much of me?" His voice shook. His chin quivered. "You really want me to become part of Everhide?"

"Yes," the three of us said in sync, then laughed.

"It's up to you, Hayds." Hunter scrunched up the wrapper from his lunch and tossed it into the takeaway bag. "There is a lot to consider—the additional fame, the shitty paparazzi, needing bodyguards, having to hang out with us more often, and the big bonus ... more money and royalties."

"Oh my God." Hayden raked his fingers through his short brown hair, leaving tousled tracks in their wake. "I honestly never expected this. We discussed the potential of one day being involved in the songwriting process when you hired me. But to be the fourth member of Everhide? That's fucking *INSANE.* You don't have to do this. Just give me the music and I'd be happy. I don't need to walk the red carpet or be on album covers, or at interviews. I just love drumming."

"Bullshit." I cough-laughed. "Yes, you love music as much as we do. But you love the attention too. You craved it when you were with The Saylors. Now, you've earned it. You're getting recognized when you go out. You share the stage with us anyway, so you may as well share the spotlight. This is the perfect time to bring you into the front line—before we write and release the singles or start the album. Unless . . ." My heart faltered. ". . . you're planning on going somewhere else?"

"Um . . . no." He jerked his chin back. "Not ever. But fuck . . . This exceeds anything I've ever dreamed of. Oh, wow!" He clutched his drumsticks against his chest. "This is amazing. I have to talk to Lex; I'm sure she won't hesitate. But more than anything, I think you've given me the most compelling reason to convince her we finally can, and have to, move."

"You want to move?" Kyle scratched his cheek. "Where to?"

"Down this way. So we're closer to you guys. But we can only afford something cheap and nasty that's probably worse than the shoebox we live in."

Having Lexi and Hayden closer, within walking distance, would be ideal. It would make it easier to catch up for practice and to hang out with them. I didn't falter. "We could help you out . . . with a loan . . . if needed."

"I could never ask that of you guys." Shock still rocked Hayden's voice. "You've already done so much. This offer is mind-blowing as it is."

I waved in the general direction of my building. "There's an apartment coming up for sale in a few months in the complex on the other side of our place."

Hayden's eyebrows skewed, one up, one down. "Yeah. But that would be millions, Gem. We can't afford that."

"With our help, you could," Kyle added. "You can pay us back after the release of our next album."

"Fuck." Hayden rubbed the back of his neck as he stared at the ceiling. "That blows my mind."

"Cool, hey?" Hunter slapped Hayden on the thigh.

Kyle grabbed his cell phone from the front pocket of his jeans and typed himself a note. "We'll talk to our lawyer and draw up a new agreement for joining us and one for a loan. I'll get Richard to email them to you. So if all terms and conditions are agreeable, are you in, Hayds?"

I squeezed Kyle's leg and held my breath.

"Fuck. I know the terms will be exceptional. Lex will take some convincing to agree to the loan, but she won't balk at me joining you." Hayden's disbelief morphed into marvel. "I'd be crazy not to say yes. So . . . YES!"

"Ahhhh." I leaped to my feet with the guys. I rushed around the coffee table with Kyle and joined Hunter in group-hugging Hayden. Together, we jumped up and down, laughing and cheering.

Out of the many changes we'd faced, this was one of the best. We'd connected the moment we'd met, but being in different bands had kept us apart. Our friendship had intensified over the years, though. We'd been through so much together. The three of us had supported him through dealing with his drug-addicted parents; we'd played our part in bringing him and Lexi together, and we'd made his dreams come true when we'd brought him into our backup band. Now it was time to take our bond to the next level. It was time to make him one of Everhide. Easily done, since he loved music as much as we did.

With my arms linked around Kyle's and Hunter's waists, I hugged them closer. I rested my head against Kyle's arm. Our Everhide family had grown. Hayden belonged with us. And maybe . . . just maybe . . . I'd be ready for a few new little Everhide members soon too.

I was nowhere near ready to pick out baby names or nursery colors, but as long as my friendships never faltered, my love for Kyle grew stronger and stronger, and music filled my soul, I'd survive anything. Even having this baby.

Chapter 11

HAYDEN

"I don't want to look at apartments. I don't have time."

"Yes, you do." I caught the back of Lexi's office chair in our spare bedroom and spun her around to face me. I knelt in front of her and placed my hands on her knees. Stress creased her brow. Dark circles shadowed her eyes. She'd been working crazy long hours, editing footage for Everhide's new documentary and preparing initial creative briefs for their ... *our* ... new video clips. It was so cool I'd be in them. But before we got caught up in travel and more work, we needed to find a new home.

"Please? Just for a few hours." I tucked her blonde curls behind her ear. "You need a break." I stood and held out my hand.

She folded her arms and didn't budge. "I'm not moving to a new apartment. So why bother?"

Butterflies dipped and swooped in my stomach. I'd never been in a position to buy a property before. Now, I was. Moving would give us a home and foundation to start a new chapter of our life together. We'd find somewhere with room for our family. Lexi was just over two months pregnant; I wanted to find somewhere as soon as possible.

"Please." I stood my ground. I'd seen her looking over my shoulder as I'd browsed the real estate sites, looking at apartments for sale. This wasn't a total dead-in-the-water cause. "Just humor me. Come with me to look at a couple of places I've lined up for this afternoon."

It had been two weeks since Kyle, Gemma, and Hunter had asked me to frontline with them. Lexi had screamed and shrieked so loudly when I'd told her the news that everyone in Hawaii had heard her. I'd been waiting for the legal documents and details to come through. They'd arrived in my inbox this morning.

While Lexi had worked, I'd gone through every point and sub-point in the contract. My heart had pounded so hard, I'd nearly passed out twice. What Everhide had offered me had blown my mind.

It was beyond my wildest dreams.

Becoming an official part of Everhide was the beginning of a new era. *This* would set me up for life. I'd survived drug-addicted parents and foster homes and lived on rations and barely there royalties from my former band for years. I'd never forget where I'd come from—that shit had burned my brain. But it was time to look forward. Everything I'd worked so hard for had finally paid off.

Electricity charged through my veins like an overloaded circuit.

I had to get Lexi on board to move.

With only one shot at the element of surprise, I prayed I could pull off my plan. I had to keep my *chomping-at-the-bit* heartbeat on a leash—I didn't want it to run away. I had to play it cool, act normal.

"Lex." I shook my held-out hand again. "Please come. I don't want to keep the agent waiting."

She slumped her shoulders and slapped her palm into my hand. "Fine. But nothing will sway me."

"Okay."

"You think that because you're gonna make a bit more money now, you can blow it all on a condo?"

A bit? She had no idea.

Ever since Lexi's parents' bitter divorce and their cruel bickering over every dime, Lexi had been budget-conscious and cautious with her money. She'd kept me in line. I was much more precarious, but not downright frivolous. *Well . . . only sometimes.* But it was nice that I no longer had to worry about when or where my next paycheck was coming from.

I grabbed my cell phone and jacket, then picked up her purse and coat, and handed them to her. "We're just looking, not signing our lives away." *But hopefully we will.*

We jumped into an Uber and headed south.

The first three-bedroom condo in Soho was smaller than our current apartment. I hadn't thought that was possible. The photos on the Internet had been deceiving. It was instantly not a contender.

As we entered the second apartment on Sullivan Street, Lexi wrinkled her nose. "What is that smell?"

The three-bedroom place was open-plan and full of natural light. But it only had one bathroom, had to be accessed via two flights of narrow stairs, and a horrid smell of acetone permeated each room.

"Is that stench nail polish? Coming from the salon downstairs?" I wrinkled my nose. I didn't mind the smell, but I didn't want to live with it on a daily basis.

Lexi placed her hand on her stomach, and the color drained from her face. "I'm not sure if it's because I'm pregnant, but it's making me sick." She closed her eyes and swallowed hard, like she was about to vomit. "This is a no. I can't live with that odor. Let's get out of here. Please?"

"I'm with you."

Lexi slumped in the back seat of the Uber and sighed as if she were tired and weary. "Can we go home now? This is pointless."

I clutched and squeezed her hand. "After one more place, I promise."

"Whatever." She stared out the window.

The drive to the next location only took a few minutes.

Lexi's eyes widened when we stopped outside the building next to Kyle and Gemma's place. "What are we doing here?"

"There's a condo in here to look at."

"But . . . we can't afford anything in a place like this. It would cost millions, right? We don't have that kind of money. Two years ago, we could barely pay our monthly rent. We're better off now working for our friends and have some savings put aside, but there is no way the bank would give us a loan for this much. We couldn't afford the mortgage."

I helped her out of the car. "Let's just look at it. For fun."

She rolled her eyes and grumbled. "You're wasting my time."

"Come." I dragged her toward the building. "Where's your sense of adventure?"

"At home. Planning *your* video shoots."

Wicked. But that could wait.

"I'll take you home straight after this. I promise." I gave her a quick kiss on the lips, then opened the door and led her inside.

The building manager I'd arranged to meet was waiting for us.

"Mr. and Mrs. Moore. Nice to meet you. I'm Breanna." Her face lit with a friendly smile as she held out her hand.

I shook it, and so did Lexi.

Breanna didn't look much older than us. Dressed in a gray designer suit and high heels, with just a hint of make-up on, Breanna had hundreds of tiny black braids pulled back into a long ponytail that fell to her waist. She seemed much more approachable than the *I'm-only-in-it-for-the-commission* agent who had shown us the previous places.

"Let's head on up, shall we?" Breanna waved toward the elevators. "The condo is on the fifth floor. It isn't listed on the market yet. The owners are moving to Dubai in a couple of months and would like to sell privately."

"So, Hayds." Lexi tugged on my arm as we stepped inside the elevator and headed upward. "How did you find out about this place?"

I leaned in and whispered in her ear. "I have my sources."

"But . . ." Lexi's voice trailed off as the elevator doors opened.

Bright lights blazed down on a bunch of fresh flowers in a huge gold vase centered on a console table. Rectangular mirrors lined the walls. Our shoes clicked on the glossy beige tiles as Breanna led us toward the apartment door. This beat the hell out of the dingy, dark hallway in our building. Breanna entered a code into a security pad and let us into the condo.

The moment I stepped inside and left my shoes by the door, warmth settled on my skin. Lexi gaped and gawked at the open-plan room. Sprawling black-framed windows gave way to views of the narrow tree-lined street. Pale oak floors highlighted the black cabinets and marble countertops in the gourmet kitchen. A navy L-shaped sofa faced the largest wall-mounted flat-screen TV I'd ever seen. I could picture our kids jumping on the furniture, having sliding contests on the floorboards, and eating breakfast at the kitchen island. I curled my toes inside my socks. Or maybe I just wanted to do those things with Lexi.

After Breanna ran through the square footage, condo features, and building details, she pointed toward the bedrooms. "Wander through. Take your time. I'll wait over here by the windows."

Taking Lexi's hand, I led her down the hall. We peered into two large bedrooms with high ceilings, plush cream carpet, and natural light flooding in through the windows. One was furnished with pale pink bedding and dolls. In the other, there were bookcases and a bed in the shape of a race car. *So cool.*

Would we have a boy and a girl? Who knew? I was just grateful that I could give my family a warm, clean, vibrant home full of love. So radically different from my upbringing.

"This place is insane," Lexi whispered as we headed across the hallway into the master bedroom.

"It's awesome." I kept my voice low too. The condo wasn't as big and flashy as Gemma and Kyle's place or as outrageous as Hunter and Kara's penthouse, but it was a gazillion times better than where we lived at present.

"Oh, wow!" Lexi stared up at the funky light of crisscrossed bars and oversized round light globes. The bedroom was bigger than our entire apartment, with a king-sized bed butted up against a velvet-padded headboard, double-width nightstands, a cozy reading nook, and a huge window that looked toward Gemma and Kyle's place.

"Holy shit." Lexi stepped inside the walk-in closet and spun around.

I followed, my feet sinking into the thick carpet. I never knew flooring could be so soft.

"I think I just died and went to heaven." Lexi scanned the built-in drawers, shoe racks, clothes railings, and shelves that spanned the walls from floor to ceiling.

I chuckled as I took in the space. It would take a lifetime to fill this closet with clothes and accessories. "It's wicked, right?"

After checking out the luxurious master bathroom with marble countertops, double basins, and a massive shower, I caught Lexi's hand. In the middle of the bedroom, I tugged her closer and wrapped my arms around her waist. "So . . .? What do you think?"

"Hayds." Bewilderment swirled in her eyes. "This condo is beautiful. But we're not rich like our friends. I know you'll be earning more money, but not this much money. We can't afford a home like this."

I linked my fingers at the base of her spine. "What if we could?"

Confusion crinkled her brow. "What are you talking about?"

My heart raced faster. "You know how we have amazing friends?"

"Yes. So?" She tilted her head to the side. Intrigue narrowed her eyes.

"They have offered us a loan. Interest-free. They know the banks won't approve this type of money for us, but they can."

"But . . . but . . . how much does this place actually cost?"

"Four point seven."

"Million?" Lexi's hand shot over her heart. "We can't ask them to do that. It's too much. We'll be paying them back forever."

"That's my second piece of news. Come sit with me." We sat on the padded bench at the end of the bed. My hand shook as I pulled my cell phone out of my jacket, swiped the screen, and opened the document I'd read through this morning. "I got the contract from Gem and the guys. I spent this morning going through some calculations. Kyle gave me some numbers to work with. Based on the royalties they earned on their last album and the tour; this is what I can expect to make in the next two to three years."

I showed Lexi the screen.

Her mouth gaped. Tears welled in her eyes. "Are you shitting me?"

"Nope." My head still spun at the sight of the six zeros at the end of the first two digits. I'd checked my spreadsheet three times to make sure my calculations were correct. This was better than winning the lottery. The royalties would continue for the rest of my life.

Lexi drew my cell toward her face and stared at the numbers. "I knew our friends were rich, but that's ludicrously rich."

"They didn't make the Forbes list of the *World's Top-Earning Musicians* twice by releasing one hit."

"I thought that was their net worth, not annual income?"

"Nope." I shook my head. "It's annual. And this number . . ." I waved my cell phone from side to side. "It doesn't include sponsorship deals or appearance fees or other gigs we might do in the future."

"Oh. My. God." A tear slid down Lexi's cheek. She clutched my arm. "I'm shaking all over. I can't comprehend that type of money."

"Neither can I. But it's happening." I swiveled to face her and took her hands in mine. Inhaling deeply, I breathed Lexi in. Her sweet perfume filled my head. She was so beautiful, my angel. She'd been my strength, my support, my saving grace for so many years. I wanted to do this for her. "I want this incredible opportunity of being a part of Everhide to be a new start for us. We're having a baby. You've got your dream job doing the band's photography and working with Clayton on the creative direction. I'm drumming for them. We've cherished our friends' generosity for so long, but now we get to stand beside them. I have loved living with you in our tiny rundown apartment and the memories it holds. But we've outgrown it. I'm not asking you to move into the flashiest condo in Tribeca, or to live beyond our means. *This* is our means." I glanced around the room and squeezed her hands. "Buying something this expensive makes me nervous, excited, and overwhelmed. I've got cold sweats and shivers." I met her gaze and wiped her damp cheek with the pad of my thumb. "But I want to give you the life you deserve. The life we've worked so hard for and can now enjoy. I want this for you, for us, for our family."

Concern loomed in the depths of her eyes. "It's so much money."

"Which we now earn. We'll be right next door to Kyle and Gem, and around the corner from Kar and Hunt. This place is perfect."

She sniffled, bit her lip, and nodded. "So, we won't have late-night taxi rides and Uber fares home?" A new shimmer of excitement sparkled in her eyes. "No subway trains or long drunk walks back to our place?"

"Nope . . . well . . . there will still be drunk walks home. They will just be very short and won't give us time to sober up."

"If our friends are loaning us this much money, should we look at other condos in the area?"

"If you want to. I have looked, but there isn't much around."

"We'd better check out a few." She scanned the room. New tears dampened her eyelashes. "But I don't think anything will top this. The second I walked in here, it felt like home. I love the layout, the finishes, the space. It's right next to our friends. It's perfect."

I'd felt a connection with the place the moment I'd stepped inside, too. Was it meant to be?

"So, is that a yes?"

Lexi lowered her chin. "I never wanted to move. I was afraid to let go of the memories because most of them are of you." Then she peered up at me from underneath her curls that had fallen across her forehead. "But I've captured them on film and have stored them in my heart. No matter where we go, they will always be with me. You're right." She entwined her fingers with mine. "We're financially in a different place now. We can afford something better. I wasn't expecting this much of a leap, but I'm willing to take it with you."

My heart swelled, beating like a bass drum. "You mean that?"

"Yeah." She ran her hand up my thigh, then jabbed her finger against the muscle. "Just don't break your fucking arm or leg or something that would stop you playing the drums for them, or we'll be really screwed. If we have to rely on my income, we *will* be paying Everhide off for the rest of our days."

"I'll try not to." I caught her hand and clutched it tight. "So? Are we gonna buy a home?"

A smile curled across her lips. "You've finally worn me down. So, yes. Let's buy a condo. Let's look at some others, but I think I want *this* one."

I leaped to my feet and dragged Lexi to stand. I wrapped my arms around her and kissed her hard. Every time I kissed her, I loved her more and more. From the moment I'd told her I loved her on a walk home late at night a few years ago, to the first time we'd made love after the Jingle Ball in Washington, to the night she came to Boston and fought for my heart, to our wedding day, our life had gotten better and better. We'd had bold dreams, worked hard at our jobs, and we'd had many ups and downs. But we'd survived because we had each other and an incredible circle of friends. With a baby on the way, and exciting careers and adventures ahead of us, finally, all of our New York dreams had come true.

Chapter 12

HUNTER

"TWINS!" My jaw hit the floor. I stared at our doctor. My heart clawed my face. "Did you say, *twins*?"

Dr. Arnold nodded as she ran the probe across Naomi's abdomen.

"Oh my God." Sitting beside me, Kara squealed and squeezed my hand. Her leg knocked and nudged against mine as she tapped her feet. Her smile was as bright as the sun.

"Oh, fuuuuck!" Naomi glared at the ultrasound image on the monitor. "Are you sure?" She clutched her rumpled blouse beneath her breasts so hard her knuckles turned white.

"Yes." Dr. Arnold positioned the probe low on Naomi's abdomen and pointed at the screen. "Here is one fetus. And tucked to the left is the other. Two little heartbeats going strong."

"I didn't sign up for twins." Naomi's hand trembled as she brushed her brow.

I closed my eyes. My pulse pounded in my temples. *Twins!*

The past several weeks since Naomi had confirmed she was pregnant had flown by with songwriting, recording, marketing meetings, fittings, selecting directors for our video clips, and savoring time spent with Ashleigh and Kara. My mind still spiraled at the fact that three of my favorite women on the planet were pregnant—Gemma, six months; Lexi, four months; and Naomi, twelve weeks. Watching them grow babies coiled warmth around my heart. Through it all, Kara had remained stoic. Even though it killed her not carrying our baby, I'd never seen her so happy. She doted on the girls' every need, brought them gifts, pampered them, shared baby product catalogs, and gave advice on must-have items, all while being an amazing mother to our daughter. She thrived in motherhood. She'd grown stronger, healthier, and happier. But was she ready for this? For twins?

I had wanted to expand our family, but with *twins*?

Holy. Fucking. Shit.

Excitement and bewilderment danced in Kara's eyes. She clutched Naomi's hand. "You knew it was a risk when you signed up to be our surrogate. There was a chance the embryo could split."

"Yeah . . . but—"

"Too late now." A cold sweat broke out on the back of my neck. Fevered blood charged through my veins. If all went according to plan, and Naomi didn't miscarry again, Kara and I would have three children under the age of two before Christmas. *Fuck! THREE!*

"This is so incredible." A tear caught on Kara's cheek. "I never thought I'd have one baby. Now, we might have another two." She flicked the droplet off her cheek with her fingertips. But an undercurrent of reserve rippled through her tone. After the troubles and the tragedies we'd gone through, from losing Ryan to two surrogate miscarriages, we knew not to get our hopes up until we held our baby in our arms. Well, now . . . would it be *babies*?

"This is insane." I wiped my hand down my face, then tapped my cheek to make sure I wasn't dreaming. "Are they healthy? Are they doing okay?"

Dr. Arnold nodded. "Yes. They are a good size. The heartbeats are strong. Would you like to know their gender?"

I clutched Kara's hand, lifted it to my mouth, and kissed the back of it. "Do you want to keep it a surprise like we did with Ashleigh?" We didn't find out about her. It had made the moment so much more amazing. Hearing 'It's a girl,' and the sound of Ashleigh's first cry would be embedded in my memory for all time.

"Um . . . no," Kara whispered. "A surprise is good."

But deep down, not knowing made it easier to deal with any potential loss. There was still a long way to go.

Another tear meandered down Kara's cheek. "Is that okay?"

"Yeah. I'm down with that." I leaned over and kissed her lips; they were salty from her tears. When I drew back, the mix of happiness, elation, fear, and hope swirling in her eyes reflected my own concerns. But the sheer horror on Naomi's face made me chuckle. "Nae? You okay?"

"No. I've changed my mind." Naomi shook her head. "Can I renege on this whole surrogacy deal?" Her voice quaked, half serious, half joking. "I'm gonna end up as huge as Harlem."

"You'll be fine." Kara stroked her sister's hair. "You carried Ashleigh for us. We have faith in you."

Naomi's head sank deeper into the pillow. "I'm so glad this is the last time."

"Me too." I nodded. Three kids would be more than enough. "This is it, Nae. It's the last chance for us to have a biological child . . . I mean, children." *Wow! Twins.*

"Great," Naomi grumbled. "No pressure."

"None." I gave her a reassuring smile. "What will be, will be." We'd learned that the hard way and had the scars on our hearts from our battles. But Kara and I had survived and had a beautiful daughter thanks to never giving up on our dreams . . . and thanks to Naomi for being our surrogate.

"Everything looks good and is on track." Dr. Arnold cleaned the gel off her probe with a paper towel and handed a handful of tissues to Naomi to wipe the goo off her belly. "We're all done for now. With twins, we like to monitor their progress closely. I'll want to see you every four weeks. Naomi, you may make full term and have a natural birth, but in many cases, we have to extract the babies sooner by cesarean. We'll know closer to the due date."

If we make it that far.

"I'm happy either way." Naomi swung her feet off the bed and realigned her blouse. "As long as they're healthy."

So true.

"I'll do my best to ensure they are." Dr. Arnold stood and shook our hands. "It's good to see you again, and glad to hear Ashleigh is doing well. We love surrogacy success stories." She waved toward the door. "Please see the receptionist on the way out and schedule your appointments."

"Will do." Kara picked up her purse and hooked it over her shoulder.

The moment we stepped out of Dr. Arnold's office, Kara yanked on my hand, nearly ripping it from its socket, and danced a happy jig. "Oh, Hunt. Twins? Can you believe it? This is amazing."

My heart raced as I wrapped my arms around her, picked her up, and twirled her around. I placed her back on her feet and hugged her. "It's a huge shock. But yeah. It's incredible." The full concept of having twins hadn't sunk in yet, but an addition—now two—to our family was what we'd wanted. They were our babies. My DNA and Kara's. That was phenomenal. I caught Kara's face between my hands and kissed her lips, savoring the taste of her strawberry-flavored lip gloss. "I think we're gonna have to celebrate."

The wickedly hot *we're-gonna-have-a-baby* sex we'd had after I'd agreed to have our first child flickered through my mind. *Mmm.* We had to get out of there, quick.

Kara's cheeks flushed a deep shade of red. Hunger flared in her eyes. "I like the sound of that."

Good. She'd read my mind.

"But we have to catch a plane." She winced.

Damn it.

"Are you two done?" Naomi leaned against the reception counter. "I've made the appointments. I've added them to your calendars." She glanced at her watch. "I've got to get back to the office. Is it all right if we say goodbye here?"

"Yes. Absolutely." Kara bounded forward with her arms held

wide. "We've got to get to the airport, anyway."

"Sorry, I can't come with you." She hugged Kara, then me. "I'm too busy this week at work. I'll see you on the weekend for Ashleigh's birthday."

"Will do." I stuffed my hands into the back pockets of my jeans and half-grinned. "We might need to charter a flight home to carry all the crap Kar has bought for her." Kara had planned a huge first birthday for Ashleigh in LA, sparing no expense on the venue, the party planner, catering, cake, and decorations, as well as an insane number of presents. She'd already bought a ton of toys and trinkets from Tiffany and more clothes than I owned . . . and I had a lot of clothes. My kid was already more of a fashionista than Kara and me combined. Considering most of our LA friends didn't have kids, I was convinced Kara just wanted an excuse to show off our daughter. And I was totally down with that. "I don't know why a baby needs so much stuff."

"Because she's worth it." Kara raised one shoulder and fluttered her eyelashes.

I couldn't argue with that. "Come on. We have to go."

I took Kara's hand, rushed her out of the building and into our waiting car. As our driver pulled out into the traffic, Kara straddled my lap. Her long skirt gathered around her hips.

Now this was good.

Her lips found mine. Her hands threaded through my hair and clutched it. "I think we need to celebrate now."

"Mmm." I groaned as she rubbed her crotch against my groin. *Instant boner.* "If you insist."

"For fuck's sake," Mick, my bodyguard, mumbled from the front passenger seat. "Can't you wait until you're home?" He hit a button and the blackout divider screen shut to give us privacy.

I tilted my head back and chuckled. "I secretly think he likes to watch."

"I'm sure he has," Kara whispered against my lips. "I don't care."

"Fuck, I love you."

I drew her lips to mine. As I slid my hand over the curve of her breast, down her hip, and along her smooth leg, my fingertips tingled. I needed more of her bare flesh against mine. As I slipped my hand beneath her skirt, fire coiled through my veins. I wanted to yank off her clothes, tease her torturously. Adore every inch of her body. The possibility of more children, fulfilling Kara's dreams, and falling in love with her more each day filled me with an uncanny joy. Four years ago, I would've never pictured myself married with children. But now, there was nothing I wanted more than a life with Kara, our kids, and music. They were everything. *She* was everything.

As I trailed my fingers over the front of her silky panties, blood rushed to my cock. Her arousal had dampened the soft fabric. I loved it when she was turned on, hot and hungry. Our kisses deepened. Our breaths entwined. But just as I slipped my finger underneath the edge of her panties, her cell phone rang. Diego's ringtone buzzed from her purse.

Kara ignored it, rocking her pussy against my touch. "Don't stop."

But her cell rang again. Diego only did that if it was an emergency.

"Shit." Kara slid off my lap, leaving my hard-on throbbing, aching, and begging to be released from my boxer briefs. I winced, clutching my dick to ease the agony as Kara dived into her purse. She grabbed her cell phone and answered it, tapping the screen to put it on speaker. "Diego?" She swept her hair off her brow. Her voice was a breathy fluster. "What's up?"

"It's Ashleigh. Quick. You need to hurry home."

The blood drained from my entire body. A chill stilled my heart. "What's happened?"

"Just. Come. Quick." Diego's voice was shrill, ringing through the speaker, then he hung up.

"What the fuck?" Kara had turned as white as paper. She dialed Diego's number. Fear darkened her eyes. Her hand trembled. "Hunt, he's not answering."

"Shit." I leaned forward and slapped my hand against the divider. I pressed the button to lower the screen. "Something's wrong with Ashleigh. Get us the fuck home. Now!"

Chapter 13

HUNTER

Our driver made it to my building in record time. I grabbed Kara's hand, and we rushed inside. Fear gripped my heart as we raced up to our floor in the elevator with Mick beside us. We bolted into the living room and skidded to a halt.

Diego lowered the book he was reading to Ashleigh. His smile widened, and his eyes blazed, lively and bright.

What the...?

Ashleigh sat on her play mat, chewing on her Bright Stars Sensory Llama. She didn't look hurt or sick.

What was going on?

"Diego?" Panting, I struggled to form words. "What's the emergency?"

"This." He picked up Ashleigh, held her on her wobbly feet, and faced her toward us. He held her by the tips of her tiny fingertips. "Okay, Ashleigh. Show your mommy and daddy what you can do. Come on. You can do it."

Ashleigh clung to his fingertips and placed one tiny foot in front of the other. The pink bow clipped into her curls slid sideways as she wobbled. A big grin spread across her sweet little round face. Her blue eyes glittered like her sparkly top.

Then Diego let go of her hands.

With her arms held wide, Ashleigh took one step. Two steps. *Wait.* Three. Four. Five. Then she fell onto all fours and power-crawled to my feet. She sat on her haunches and raised her arms.

"Oh my God!" Kara cried, crossing her hands over her chest. "She's walking?"

My heartbeat switched from its jack-hammering panic to soaring like an eagle. I picked up Ashleigh, swept her soft curls off her face, and planted a kiss on her cheek. "Hey, princess?" *Oh, thank goodness you're okay.* "You're walking? That's so cool. You're so clever."

I swiped the dribble from her lips with my thumb and wiped it on my jeans. Baby drool and snot were my latest fashion item additions.

"Oh . . . we missed it." Kara rubbed Ashleigh's toes. "I wanted to see her first steps."

"She's only taken about ten in total." Diego sauntered over to us with his hands in his cargo pants. "I called straight away so you could get here."

"Thank you." Tears welled in Kara's eyes. She couldn't hide the disappointment that she'd missed Ashleigh's first steps nor the overwhelming relief that Ashleigh was safe. "Our little girl is on the move."

Mick held out his hand toward Diego, his eyes searching the room, the kitchen, the hallway. "So there's no emergency? No security breaches or threats?"

"No." Diego's eyebrows pinched together, but then they widened. His mouth fell open, and he clutched his chest. "Oh, no. I'm so sorry. I should be more careful with emergency calls, right?"

"Yes, please." Kara sniffled, but her gaze held a strict warning. "You scared us half to death."

After kidnappings, death threats, and tragic losses, our anxiety, stress, and paranoia constantly hovered in the backs of our minds and was easily triggered. *Fuck.* I let out a steady breath, and my pulse gradually returned to normal. My kids might be the death of me. "I'm glad you're both safe. Don't freak us out like that again."

"No, Mr. Hunter." Diego shook his head. "I'm very, very sorry. I was just so excited to see her walk." With worry darkening his eyes, his gaze darted from me to Kara, then back again. "Am I fired?"

"No. No. Not at all." Kara softened her gaze, stepped over to him, and gave him a hug. "We love you too much. In fact, we want to add to your duties. With twins."

Diego shrieked, clapped his hands, and jumped up and down. "Oh wow. That is brilliant. Congratulations."

If someone was that excited to look after five babies, he was a keeper. But conscious of time, I glanced at the wall clock. We had a plane to catch. "Diego? Are you all packed?"

"Yes. Yes." Diego pointed toward the stack of five suitcases by the dining table, along with a portable crib, a new car seat, and the stroller. "Three cases are mine. The rest of the gear is Ashleigh's."

Shit. Diego was as bad as Kara. He didn't know how to travel light. But we'd be spending the next six weeks in LA for work, so I let him off the hook.

I rocked Ashleigh in my arms and patted her diaper-covered tiny butt. "Are you ready to catch a plane, princess?" She'd already clocked up a ton of air miles. We'd been to Las Vegas, LA, and Chicago to visit my family. Kara had stayed home with her when I'd gone to London. But my daughter was destined to be a world traveler. "Daddy's got to go to work. Film some video clips. Make some music. Meet some fans."

Kara swooped in and kissed Ashleigh on the forehead, then kissed me on the cheek. She ran her hand over my ass and squeezed it hard. "Raincheck on celebrating?" Faced with no emergency at home, fire returned to simmer in her eyes.

Hmm. "For now. But we will soon. I promise." I handed Ashleigh to Kara. "We better go. I'll grab our gear."

I dashed down to our room and grabbed the suitcases we'd packed this morning and two of my guitars stowed in their cases. Mick and Diego helped cart our gear downstairs and loaded the two waiting cars.

"Traveling with kids is ridiculous," I mumbled as I shoved the last bag into the trunk. We'd need to rent a minibus when we had the twins.

"See you at the airport." Mick waved, then he and Diego headed off with the driver in the front car. Kara, Ashleigh, Giles—Kara's bodyguard—and I followed.

By the time we reached the private charter airport, the mind-boggling news of twins had overtaken my thoughts, and a barrel of excitement skipped through my system. Twins would be so cool. But *crap.* That meant two of everything—clothes, cribs, rockers, and highchairs. I loved to spend my money on fast cars, fancy clothes, fine dining, and fabulous hotels, but now I spend more cash on baby items than I'd ever thought was possible. Cuddly teddy bears, cute denim jackets, and petite pearl bracelets were must-have items. I was as bad as Kara at spoiling Ashleigh. What would I be like with twins?

After checking in our luggage for our private flight, we headed toward the VIP lounge. As Diego pushed Ashleigh ahead in her stroller, I hooked my arm around Kara's shoulders. I leaned in and whispered in her ear, "Can I claim my raincheck now?"

Our delayed celebrations had hummed like a Harley-Davidson engine between us for the entire drive here. There was nothing subtle about it.

"Shh." Kara blushed as we walked through the glass doors into the lounge. "Stop teasing, or we'll end up in trouble."

Fire coiled through my veins. "I like trouble."

"Later."

"Spoilsport." I took her hand in mine and kissed the inside of her wrist as we walked toward our friends, lazing on the sofas. Our entourage had flown out to LA earlier in the day.

"Hunt?" Gemma jumped to her feet, tugging her shirt over her bulging baby bump, and rushed forward to greet us. She didn't let being six months pregnant slow her down. She still liked to deny that the baby was happening. "You're late." Concern shot through her tone. "Is Nae okay? Is the baby all right?"

I placed my hands on her shoulders to steady myself, to regather my wandering mind. "Yes . . . but . . . it's bab*ies*."

"Oh, shit." Kyle leaped from his seat and joined Gemma. He chuckled and slapped me on the back. "Congratulations . . . but *twins*?"

"Yep." Kara curled her hand around my arm and nudged her hip against my side. "It's daunting, scary . . . but very exciting."

As she turned into me, her breasts brushed against my bicep. She teased her nipple against my arm. *Fuck!* Total torture.

She winked at me and smiled. *Yeah.* She knew what she was doing. Knew the effect she had on me. "We can't wait."

I couldn't wait to commemorate the occasion. Every smoldering glance, every tender touch from Kara had my nerves begging for more. I needed to get her alone. To revel in our news and count our blessings.

Damn. This could be a fun flight to LA or one of pure agony. She wasn't making it easy for me.

Lexi ambled over to us as she rubbed her hand over her belly. "One baby at a time is enough for me. I'm as big as a baboon already."

"Angel." Hayden stepped in beside her. His mouth quirked into a half-smile. "You're four months. You're supposed to be showing. But I can start calling you 'Monkey' if you wish."

She jabbed her finger against his chest and narrowed her gaze. "Don't even think about it."

Gemma giggled and rolled her eyes, then stepped in to hug Kara and then me. "Congratulations. We pray it all goes well."

"Thanks, Gem." I ruffled the top of her head. "So do we."

High heels clicking on the hard floor caught everyone's attention. A lady in a navy pantsuit strode toward us and greeted us with a bright, red-lipped smile. "Excuse me, everyone. Your plane is ready for boarding. Please, follow me."

We grabbed our gear, jackets, purses, and backpacks. Kara took Ashleigh from Diego, and we headed onto our private jet.

Once we'd boarded and taken off, and Ashleigh had fallen

asleep with Diego, I sank onto the leather seat next to Kara. Peace and quiet at last. Kyle and Gemma were quick to claim the bedroom at the rear of the plane to catch some sleep. But by the look in Gemma's eyes, they wouldn't be getting much rest. Hayden and Lexi lazed on the lounge up ahead, across from Diego, and were engrossed in watching movies. Security sat toward the front of the plane in the next section.

I pressed the call button for the flight attendant and ordered some drinks. Moments later, Kara and I held glasses of JD.

Finally, some alone time with my wife.

I clinked my glass against hers. "To twins."

"To babies." Her smile was as breathtaking as a star-filled night. She let her head fall back against the chair. "Poor Diego. He's gonna have his hands full with potentially five kids to look after."

I downed my drink, then placed the empty glass in the cupholder. "Right now, I don't want to think about Diego. We're on a private plane. Everyone is otherwise engaged. I have you to myself. We need to celebrate our news."

"I couldn't agree more." Her eyes blazed with heat. Her voice was barely audible. "I've waited all afternoon. What did you have in mind?"

I twisted toward her, ran my hand up the outside of her calf, dragging her long skirt up to her knees. "Take off your panties."

She giggled, a touch too breathy. "But Lex and Hayds are just up there. So is Diego."

They had noise-canceling headphones on, and their backs were toward us. "They won't notice or care."

"But—"

"Shh." I kissed her lips, her cheek, the tender spot beneath her earlobe. "Take them off, or I'll do it for you."

She squirmed, the plush leather seat squelching behind her back. She always wriggled when turned on.

I fell onto my knees in front of her. "I want that bare pussy of yours against my mouth. I want to taste you. Touch you. Make you come. Really. Really. Hard."

Her breath quickened. Her lips parted. "Hunt."

There was just enough room between the bay of seats in front of me to move unhindered. I slid my hands up her long, smooth legs, slipped them underneath her skirt, and caught hold of her panties. "We're gonna have more babies. Just the thought of more kids drives you wild. Now, are you going to be a good girl or a bad one? I'm hoping for option two."

"Shit." She glanced toward the galley. "What if the attendant comes?"

"Let her watch." I tugged Kara's panties down, dragged them over her knees, and pulled them from her feet. *Hmm, pale pink lace. So hot.*

I tucked them into my pocket, then eased her skirt higher and higher up her legs. I dipped my head and kissed the inside of her thigh. The smell of her rose-scented skin filled my head. "Want me to stop?"

Her fingernails combed through my long hair, sending shivers down my spine. She hooked her leg over my shoulder and sank deeper into the wide seat. "God, no."

I threw her a wicked grin, then pressed soft kisses, took playful bites, and made tiny nips against her flesh, heading closer and closer to her sweet spot. Her cool skin quivered beneath my fiery lips. Her soft moans sent blood surging to my dick. I ached to be inside her. My heart beat for her. Her pleasure. Her happiness. Her smile. She was over the moon about the twins—I wanted to give her the heavens.

Curling my hand around her leg where it rested on my shoulder, I dug my fingers into her thigh. With my other hand, I teased her pussy and dipped a finger inside her. *Mmm. So wet and warm.* Lowering my head, I dragged my tongue up the length of her slit, then licked my lips. The salty taste of her arousal was as enticing as top-shelf whiskey. I needed another shot; one hit was never enough. I circled my tongue over her clit, licked, teased, and tormented her.

This . . . was heaven.

She pulsed her pussy against my mouth, rocking her hips in time with the flicks of my tongue. "Oh, shit." Her soft, gentle moans were music to my ears. "That's. So. Good."

I'd learned what made her body quake, what rendered her speechless, how to make her come quickly or drag it out until she begged me to let her orgasm. I'd never known any woman's body like hers. I'd found home. She was mine. Forever.

"Oh, babe. That's it. There." One of her hands clutched the armrest like it was a life raft. The other clawed at the seat. "Ooooh, shit." She grabbed a handful of my hair and pulled my head back.

"Ow! What the fuck?" Had she just scalped me?

She swung her leg off my shoulder and lowered her skirt. Her face paled as she pointed. "The flight attendant."

Crap. I had a hard-on as big as the jet plane. *Fuck.* I rose to my feet, grabbed Kara's hand, and dragged her down the aisle toward the bathroom. I pulled her inside, slammed the door shut, and locked it.

Kara giggled. "That was close."

"I wouldn't have stopped." I cupped her face and kissed her. "But I don't plan on the interruption ruining our fun."

"Neither do I."

The luxurious bathroom was ten times bigger than a normal plane's, complete with a shower, toilet, and a marble-topped basin. *Hmm.* So many options.

She wrapped her arms around my shoulders and claimed my lips with hers. *Damn.* I loved it when she wanted me. It made me lose my mind.

She unbuttoned and yanked off my button-down shirt and tossed it on the floor. Then, she unzipped my jeans, drove her hand into my boxer briefs, and took hold of my rock-hard cock. *Yeah, baby.*

Fumbling with the buttons on her blouse, I came close to ripping the fucking thing off. *Stupid buttons.* Once undone, I cupped her breast and dragged the edge of her lacy bra to the side. I lowered my head and took her nipple in my mouth.

"Oh, Hunt." She arched her back toward me, driving her tit into my mouth as she pumped my cock harder.

The plane swayed and dipped in a small turbulence—or was that just the way Kara made my head spin? I flicked my tongue over her taut nipple and grinned. Yeah, this was going to be hard and fast. My balls needed to explode.

Taking hold of her arms, I spun her around and guided her toward the length of countertop next to the sink. Standing behind her, I eased her elastic-waisted skirt down to her ankles, wrapped my hand around her knee, and lifted it up. As she rested her knee on top of the counter, her hips turned slightly to the side. I loved she was nearly as tall as I was. Made fucking her so hot when our bodies aligned and our mouths and hearts connected.

I kissed down the side of her neck, slid her blouse off, then her bra. *Mmm.* As I took in her naked reflection in the mirror, heat coursed through my veins. I raked my gaze over her perfect breasts, her hard nipples, flat tummy, and bare pussy. *So beautiful.* Our eyes met. Her breath quickened. Her glistening lips parted.

The want in her eyes nearly made me come undone.

I hooked her hair back, nipped her neck, then tugged on her earlobe. "Do you see what I see? How gorgeous you are? How I love everything about you?"

"I see you. Me." She twisted her head and kissed me. "And how much you drive me crazy."

"We're perfect for each other." I ran my fingers over her bare shoulders, down her arms, and across her naked butt. Goosebumps danced across her skin in the wake of my touch.

I tore off my jeans and boxer briefs and kicked them aside. Edging in behind her, I nudged my erection against her butt cheek. Heat sizzled in the air as my body craved hers. As I planted kisses on her shoulder and neck, I slid my hand around to her front and glided my fingertips over my name tattooed beneath her breast. Her ink. True commitment. True love. True devotion. I was hers *forever.* Easing upwards, I cupped her soft flesh and teased her nipple.

Fevered waves rushed over my body as her eyes followed my every move.

"Do you like watching me touch you?"

"Mmm." Her voice rumbled softly in her throat. "I just like you touching me."

"So do I." I ran my palm across her stomach, over her hip, and down her buttock. With her knee up on the counter, I slipped my hand between her legs from behind. My heart hammered as I eased my fingers into her pussy and rubbed her back and forth. *Fuck yes.* Her eyes fluttered closed as I circled her clit, then dipped into her arousal. Slowly, I pushed and pulsed my fingers inside her. Her warm sleekness, gentle moves, and little moans drove me wild. *So. Fucking. Hot.* "It makes me so fucking hard." I tilted my hips toward her, nudging her with my cock.

She slapped her hand against the mirror and caught her bottom lip between her teeth. Fire blazed in her eyes. "Hunt. Please."

Yep. There was no way I could hold on. I grabbed my cock and guided it toward her sweet pussy. With a thrust of my hips, I buried myself inside her. *Oh, yes. Finally.* Heat coiled up my spine as I drove into her, penetrating deeper and deeper.

"Fuck, Pearl." Watching her in the mirror was a whole new level of hot, better than any porn. "Can you believe we're gonna have more babies? Twins?"

"Yes," she panted. Bliss washed over her face. "This is the perfect way to celebrate." She turned her head toward me, and our lips met. Our hot breaths and tongues entwined. But then, she turned back to the mirror. Her gaze locked onto mine. "Now. Fuck me. Harder."

How could I say no?

She clutched the edge of the counter as if bracing herself for my hard pounding.

I drew back an inch or two, then thrust into her. My breath hitched as she clenched around me. So tight. So hot. So fucking divine. It took all my strength to stop my knees from buckling. I thrust into her again. Deeper. Harder. Deeper. Harder. Reaching around her front, I slid my fingers between her legs and rubbed her clit.

"Oh, babe." She flicked her head back and rocked and pulsed against my cock. "There."

Her breath charged in time with mine. My gaze fell to her boobs. They were tight, swollen, perfect, jiggling in the mirror. I cupped one, dragged my thumb over her hardened peak, pinched and tweaked her nipple.

"Oh. God. Yes." Kara's eyes fluttered shut.

My thighs tensed. My jaw clenched. My body slammed into hers. Every fiber in my body screamed for release. The plane dipped and swayed. The engine hummed in my ears.

Kara's head fell back against my shoulder, and she groaned. "Oh. I'm gonna come." The biggest, sexy smile slid across her mouth as she shuddered and quaked against my chest.

The tension burst from my body. I came hard and strong, pumping into her, riding out every throb, every thrum, every thrust. My heart slammed against my ribs.

God, I loved Kara.

Falling for her, and marrying her, were two of the best things that had ever happened to me in my life. Finding someone who inspired me, loved me for who I was, and connected with me in mind, body, and soul was a true blessing.

Most people on the planet never found their soulmate. But I was convinced that out of all the universe, Kara was mine.

A lazy smile curled across her lips. Her hand slipped off the glass.

I withdrew from inside her, and she spun around to face me. "That. Was. Hot." She linked her hands behind my neck. "I rate the mirror."

I wrapped my arms around her waist and brushed my lips against hers. "Me too. I put that as one of my top five quick-fuck positions."

She arched an eyebrow. "That good?"

"Yeah. You watching me touch you and fuck you? That's a total turn-on. I can feel another hard-on coming just thinking about it."

"Well, we better run through your entire list of favorite positions so I can rank them too."

"Hmm." I slipped my hands down to her ass and tugged her close. "Deal."

Making love in bed was nice, but quickies were just downright fun. Hot. Daring. Sexy as hell.

There was a knock on the door.

"You two finished?" Lexi's muffled voice drifted from the other side of the door. "Pregnant lady out here. I need to pee. Hurry up."

Shit.

"One sec." I chuckled as I kissed Kara hard and deep on the lips. "I love you."

"And I love you. You're crazy. But that's what I love about you."

"Come on." I picked up her blouse and handed it to her. "We'd better get dressed before Lexi breaks down the door." I pulled on my jeans and handed Kara her panties I'd tucked into my pocket.

She cleaned herself up and put them on. "I hope we stay this hot for each other for the rest of our lives."

"So do I." I slipped on my shirt, flicked it straight and buttoned it up. "I'll hire ten Diegos to look after the kids if it means we keep having incredible, hot, bone-melting sex like this."

"Me too."

Hiring a nanny had been hard for Kara initially, but now, Diego had become part of our family. Diego gave me the flexibility to focus on my music, and Kara the ability to work as our stylist and return to design. It made us treasure the time we had with our daughter. We'd both adjusted to doing what we loved without giving up who we were. If anything, we were more fulfilled, more in love and more than happy.

My God.

My heart swelled, doubling in size. I tugged Kara close, smoothed my hand over her hair, and kissed her hard. Had I finally found what I'd been searching for ever since Kara and I had gotten together?

Yes. Yes, I had.

We'd found balance between our work, our family, our friends and loving each other. They were all I'd ever need.

This was living. Life was . . . fucking *brilliant!*

Chapter 14

KYLE

Powering my fingers over the strings, I strummed out a wicked beat on my bass. *Bah-bahbah-bah, bahbah-bah.* After spending half of the summer in LA in our house full of friends, then conducting a grueling two-week tour to promote our new chart-topping single, it was nice to be home. Just with Gemma. Playing our guitars in our music room, letting the rhythm and melody guide us, rule us, take us over, brought a smile to my face. In moments like this, we often created magic, constructed killer chord progressions, and wrote wicked lyrics.

I flicked my hair off my forehead and glanced at Gemma. She sat on the edge of the sofa across from me with concentration etched onto her face. Her fingers worked the strings as she slayed a riff. Her skin held a gorgeous golden tan from our lazy days spent in the Californian sunshine. Her beautiful dark-brown hair cascaded forward over her shoulder in glossy waves. Her emerald eyes glinted like she was a goddess. *My goddess.* My gaze fell lower. Her belly bulged behind her guitar. In six weeks, our baby was due. Life would change forever.

She was about to give me the greatest gift . . . a baby.

Words would never be enough to describe how much I loved her, or define the lengths I'd cross to protect her, or depict how much she meant to me. It hurt my heart that she'd had a hard pregnancy—all-day morning sickness and sore boobs—but she rarely complained, never asked for help, never wanted to inconvenience anyone. Most of the time, she refused to acknowledge she was pregnant and drowned herself in work each day.

Like now, jotting down a new song that had come to her during lunch.

But she couldn't hide anything from me.

Little smiles curled across her lips when she touched her belly when the baby kicked. In quiet moments, she patted and sang to her pregnant tummy. Over the past few months, her vibrant walk had morphed into an amble and was now a waddle, complete with stifled groans and lower back rubbing.

I constantly worried about her. Two weeks of promotion across the US had drained her energy. I was tired after traveling and the long days, so she must be exhausted.

Did she need a break? A rest? We'd been here for two hours. I didn't want her to overdo it.

But she kept working on the song. Finessing it. Tweaking it. Replaying it. One more run-through and I'd call it quits.

I closed my eyes, let the music wash over me, and listened to the new lyrics rolling off her tongue.

> *I want to be the right kind of bad for you*
> *You know I ain't a good girl*
> *Come into my world*
> *I wanna take you out for a good time*
> *Just for one night*
> *Loving you is easy*
> *Easy as breathin'*
> *But I'll be gone by the morning*
> *Don't you dare be a crying*
> *Just play by my rules*
> *'Cause*
> *I want to be the right kind of bad for you*

I caught on to her changes in the beat, quickened my strum to match her tempo, and sang the new verse we'd just penned.

I want to be the right kind of bad for you
You know I ain't a good guy
Just out for a good time
I wanna take you out dancing
A little romancing
Loving you is easy
Easy as breathin'
But I'll be gone by the morning
Don't you dare be a crying
Just play by my rules
'Cause
 I want to be the right kind of bad for you

I tapped my foot and bobbed my head. I loved where this song was heading with its sexy, provocative rhythm.

But a screech sliced through the air, obliterating my thoughts.

"Fuck!" Gemma ripped the guitar strap over her head and tossed her favorite Fender onto the seat beside her.

I ripped my bass off and rushed to her side. "What's wrong? Is it the baby?" My nerves had heightened every day. With every twinge she had, I thought she was going into labor. I'd be a wreck by the time the baby came.

She shuffled forward to the edge of her seat and pointed at her belly. "This stupid baby is in the way. I can't hold my guitar properly. My fingers are fat; they don't work like they used to. This is ridiculous."

I leaned over and talked to her bump. "Don't you listen to your mommy."

She tugged her tank top over her baby bulge. "I feel like a walrus."

I sat beside her and curled my hand around her thigh. Her short shorts showed off her sexy legs. "Good thing walruses are cool."

She slumped back onto the sofa. "I'm huge. Look at the size of this thing."

I placed my hand on her tummy and gave it a rub. It grew bigger and harder every day. So weird, but so amazing. I leaned forward and kissed her lips. "And I love you more and more every day."

She grinned and wrinkled her nose. "Is that possible?"

"Yeah. Absolutely." I scooped her hair off her brow. Tiredness hooded her eyes; their glint had faded. *Yep.* Enough music for today. We could work on the song later. Maybe now was as good a time as any to show her what I'd done for her. "I know you're not into hype about the baby, but I have a surprise for you."

"You know I don't like surprises."

"Come with me." I stood and held out my hand. "I wanna show you something."

I hauled her to her feet and led her upstairs. I turned the handle on the door to our third bedroom, the one we'd decided to prepare for the baby.

"I don't need to see our spare bedroom."

"Gem." I caught her arm to stop her from leaving. "Yes. You do. Come here."

I opened the door wider and led her into the room. Gone were the queen-sized bed, old furniture, and boxes of worn-out clothes. Now, a walnut-colored crib, matching dresser, and change table stood along the right-hand wall. A mobile of guitar-playing monkeys twirled above the crib. A new comfy recliner sat in the corner; I'd fall asleep on that in an instant. And a pile of huge stuffed animals—a giraffe, an elephant, a zebra, and a lion—graced the far corner near the walk-in closet.

Gemma let out a long, slow breath. Her fingers trembled in my hold.

Walking backward, I drew her deeper into the room. "What do you think?"

"When the hell did you do this?" Bewilderment widened her

eyes.

A sheepish grin inched across my mouth. "While we've been out around the city promoting our single over the past few days, Kara and Lexi came here with the interior designer and worked their magic. That's who I've been talking on the phone with between interviews. I've had to pick bed linen, approve stuffed animals, and finalize furniture. The girls were amazing, and they finished this off yesterday."

"Wow." Her gaze darted around the room to the wallpaper border of zoo animals playing musical instruments around the top of the beige walls, to the soft patterned rug on the center of the floor, to the cube-shaped shelves for books and toys near the window. "It's . . . great."

So why did fear loom in the depths of her eyes?

My chest ached. I wanted her to be excited. "Really? You like it? We can change it if you don't."

Her chin quivered. Tears dampened her eyelashes. "You did all this for me? For the baby?"

"Yes. I don't want you to worry about anything." I snaked my arms around her waist; my stomach pressed against our baby. I hooked my finger beneath Gemma's chin and lifted it. "I know you're scared. So am I. But aren't you just a little bit excited?"

She closed her eyes. "This . . . the room . . . just makes it real."

"Ah . . . yeah. And so does this." I placed my hands on her belly. "Soon, we're gonna meet this little one. Our kid is gonna be a rockstar, just like us."

"God help them."

A tiny kick pulsed and bulged beneath my fingertips. I grabbed Gemma's hand and placed it on her tummy where it rose and fell. I covered her fingers with my palm. "Gem, this is our baby. A piece of me and you. A sign of our love. Our strength. Our family. That is everything. You are my everything. I want you to be happy."

A tear slipped down her cheek, and she wiped it off with the back of her hand. "I'm happy because you're happy." Placing her palm on the center of my chest, she tugged on my T-shirt. "I'm terrified, nervous, anxious, freaking out in every way about how this thing is gonna come out of me. How will we fit a baby into our lives? I'm tired, hormonal, teary. My body aches and hurts. But deep down . . . yeah . . . there is a tiny bit of excitement."

"Really?" My heart skipped a beat.

"Yeah." She sniffled and wiped the tip of her nose with her fingertips. "I don't think I'll be jumping around and dancing up a storm anytime soon, but it's there, faint and distant."

"Oh, Gem." I cupped her face and kissed her lips. "You've just made my day."

"I love you." She curled her hands around my forearms. "I'm sorry I'm not baby mad like Kar."

"Don't be. I wouldn't want that. You had to come around in your own time. I would've waited for you until the end of time if needed. But I'm glad I don't have to. God, I love you."

I drew her lips to mine. Warmth spiraled through my veins. The weight that had lingered in my heart, the yearning for her to be happy about our baby, finally dissipated. *Thank you, God.*

She tapped my chest and broke our kiss. "One thing." She scanned the room, then pointed. "If you move the stuffed animals to be by the bookcase, and put the chair by the window, and swap the dresser and the change table around, that will look better and be more balanced."

"I can do that." I chuckled, eyeing the furniture. "I didn't think it looked quite right either. See? We are in tune."

"Absolutely." Her smile was small, but it meant the world to me. She tilted her head toward the crib. "I love the mobile."

"It's cool, isn't it?" I glanced at the twirling monkeys. "It plays music too."

She flattened her palm over my thudding heart. "And maybe . . . we can get a lamp in here for nighttime feeds."

I couldn't hide the jump in my heart rate. "Do you want to go shopping later? To buy some stuff for the baby? If the quantity of crap Hunt and Kara received from people is anything to go by, we won't need much. Until we know if it's a boy or a girl, we don't have to go overboard."

"Okay," she whispered. "We can do that. Can we get some baby blankets too?"

Her timid tone made my stomach flutter. She could be adorable . . . sometimes. It didn't happen too often, but when she was, my heart melted.

She wrapped her arms around my neck. "I want shit I like, not random crap from well-wishers."

That was more like my Gemma.

I chuckled as I stroked her soft cheek with the pad of my thumb. "We can get anything you want. Hmm . . . does this mean you're nesting, Gem?"

"No." She was quick to shake her head. "Just practical." She toyed with the back of my hair with soft and gentle strokes. "I can honestly say there's no overwhelming, warm, fuzzy feelings going on inside me for the baby—they're only faint and subtle. But for you, they're totally crazy."

"Yeah?" I dipped my head, smiled against her lips, and traced the side of her nose with the tip of mine. "How crazy?"

"Very." She slid her hands down my chest and stomach, slipped them beneath my T-shirt, and dragged her fingertips across my abs. I flinched and twisted. Even after years of being together and her constant touch, I was still ticklish as hell. A devilish glint flickered in her eyes. "One thing this baby hasn't done is ruin my appetite for you." Her fingers traveled lower, then undid the tie on my sports shorts.

I smoothed my hands over her long hair. "I am very glad about that."

"Wanna christen the baby's room?"

"You don't have to ask me twice." I grabbed the bottom of her tank top and ripped it over her head and tossed it on the floor. Her gorgeous hair fell forward over her black bra; her swollen breasts bulged out the top. Heat blazed in my fingertips as I trailed light strokes over her shoulders, across her collarbones and down the center of her chest. I carefully caressed each cup of her bra. "One thing I love about you being pregnant is the size of your tits."

"I thought you liked my small boobs."

"Hell yeah. But it's nice to enjoy these while I can."

"They hurt like hell."

Conscious of her sore nipples, I unclipped her bra, slid the straps off her arms, and dropped it beside her top. "I'll be gentle. I promise."

"You know I don't like it gentle." She yanked down my shorts and boxer briefs.

I took a breath to steady myself and kept my heart in check. She was my sun; I radiated around her. Her warmth, her touch, her smile were my reasons for living. I closed the gap between us. My erection nudged against her belly. Chuckling, I pressed my forehead against hers. "That feels weird, right?" Headbutting my baby.

Her eyes smoldered as she ran a fingernail down my fine happy trail and took hold of my hard cock. She rubbed her hand up and down my length and teased the tip with her thumb. "It feels perfectly fine to me."

My knees weakened with every stroke. Threading my hands into her hair, I dipped my head to kiss her. "Are you sure you don't want to go to our bedroom so you're more comfortable?"

"No. I'm fine." She sank onto the rug. "Just come down here."

I lowered onto my knees and eased off her shorts and panties. Stretching out naked beside her, I glided my hand up her smooth leg, over her round belly, then caressed the side of her neck. Our lips met. Long, hot kisses were fueled by the swirls of our tongues. Each taste of her mouth, each touch of her hand, each tease of her warm breath was like home. "You're my forever, Gem." I swept her hair back off her face, whispered against her lips, "I love you more than my own life."

"I feel the same way." She placed my hand on her belly. "We've created life. This is how much I love you."

Tears welled in my eyes. As I touched her tummy, the tiny kicks from our baby jolted my heart. Kissing Gemma was like indulging in a designer drug designed just for me—there was no better high. She was my addiction. Every time we made love, we grew closer. Our souls had fused together years ago. We had bonded as one, united on all fronts. Nothing could ever tear us apart.

With the lightest of strokes, I trailed my fingertips over her breast, then circled her nipple. "Is this okay?"

"Yeah." Her voice was a whispery pant. "But I want all of you."

She hooked her leg over my hip, wriggled closer, but her belly jabbed into my stomach. In the past two days, it seemed like our baby had doubled in size. After shuffling and angling around on the rug, trying to connect our bodies, we burst out laughing.

"Babe, this isn't working." Gemma giggled over our kisses. "Let me roll over."

She turned onto her other hip, her back to my chest. But as I shuffled in behind her, she groaned. "Ow! No. Lying on this side hurts my tummy without cushions or pillows." She laid on her back, bent her knees, and waggled her finger for me to crawl between her legs. "Try this way again. Like we did the other week. Where I put my legs on your shoulders."

My pulse jumped seven notches. *Oh yeah. That was good.* "The X-file?" I'd researched every way to have sex while she was pregnant to ensure she was comfortable.

"Yeah. That one."

I kissed her hard and deep, then rose onto my knees and shuffled across the floor. As I ran my hands over her legs, I edged between her thighs. She lifted one tiny foot into my hand. I kissed along the length of her leg, placed her ankle on my shoulder, and repeated the motion for the other one. I shuffled closer, sat on my haunches, and teased her glistening pussy with my cock. Gemma's eyes fluttered closed. Her hair fanned around her face. Her boobs and baby belly loomed before me. I placed my hand on her tummy and gave it a gentle rub. "My God, you are gorgeous from every angle."

A smile curled across her lips. Then she wrinkled her nose and wriggled her pussy against my dick. "Just . . . get . . . in me."

Heat pooled on the tip of my cock. It begged to be inside her. "God, Gem, you kill me. You know that?"

"Yep." She rubbed against me again. "Kyle. In. Now."

The command in her voice ignited my heart and sent fire hurtling through my veins. I loved it when she got bossy. With a tilt of my hips, I drove into her hot, wet pussy. Her warmth engulfed me as I gently thrusted in and out. In and Out. *Oh, yeah.* Sparks shot across my skin. My breath quickened. Being inside her was the best feeling. Being connected with her heart, her spirit . . . was even better.

I held onto her knees and drove into her deeper. "Is this okay? Not too hard?" I didn't want to hurt the baby. *Was that a thing?* But I didn't want Gemma to be uncomfortable either. My dick was nowhere near small.

"No. It's good." Her voice came out low and breathy. "Really good."

As I ran my hands over her silky legs, heat blazed beneath my fingertips. But her warm arousal, and her insides clenching around me, stole my focus. I widened my knees, thrust harder, plunging and driving into her faster.

One of her hands caressed her belly; the other slapped the rug and clawed into the plush wool. "Oh, yeah," she moaned. "That's so good. More. Like that."

Jeezus. If I went slow, I could savor this endearing moment with Gemma and our baby. But going fast was damn hot and fun. And Gemma liked her fun.

I licked the tip of my thumb, then pressed it against her clit. Fire and ice sizzled through my fingers as I teased and touched her.

Her hips bucked and rolled in gentle waves. Her gaze locked onto mine. She slid her hands over her belly, then caressed her breasts, massaged them and played with them.

Fuck!

She tweaked her nipples, and a soft groan rumbled low in her throat.

So hot.

Oh crap. I was gonna come. I closed my eyes and held on.

An inferno blazed in my heart. She filled my head with giddiness. "Gem?"

"Harder."

Shit.

I thrust into her depths. Every muscle in my thighs burned. Every breath seared my lungs. Her core clenched around my cock. Tighter. Tighter. Tighter.

With one deep plunge, I buried myself inside her. Unable to hold on a second longer, I spilled into her, pulsing, throbbing, thrumming. "Fuck. Yeah." My heart thudded and thumped against my ribs. Sweat licked my skin, but I didn't relent.

I rocked into her until her back arched. I touched her until her body quivered and quaked. I drove into her until she smiled and laughed.

"Oh. Wow." She panted and puffed, her chest rising and falling. A sexy glint shimmered in her gorgeous eyes.

I didn't want our orgasms to end. I pulsed inside her, letting her ride out her pleasure. Let every shiver and shudder linger.

Giggling, she eased her legs off my shoulders and drew me forward. I collapsed onto the rug beside her. She combed her fingers through my hair and kissed my lips. "That was freaking amazing."

As I caught my breath, I draped my arm over her waist. The sweet floral scent of her skin filled my senses. "You're no dainty flower."

"Never."

"I didn't bring on labor, did I? You're not having any weird pains?"

"No."

I smoothed my hand over her tummy, our baby. Gazing into her gorgeous green eyes, I smiled. Overcome with emotion, I softened my voice. "You're so beautiful. I love you so much. I know I say that a lot. But I mean it with every beat of my heart. Every time I look at you, I can't believe you're mine. Every day, I cherish this amazing life we have together. And now . . . we're gonna have a baby. Be a family. *You* have made me the happiest man alive."

She entwined her fingers with mine and held them against her chest. "I feel the same way about you. Promise me we'll do whatever it takes to be awesome parents? I wanna be a good mom. I want our kid to know we will do everything within our power to give them a great life. That we will never hurt them. Or leave them. And we will always tell them and show them we love them every single day of our existence."

Our upbringing had scarred us for life. But we'd do this family thing right. We'd love our child, no matter what. Together.

I kissed her hand and chuckled. "I think we certainly just showed them."

"That we did." She drew my mouth to hers and kissed me, slow and sweet. "I love you. Forever."

"And ever."

I could stay here all afternoon, but we had dinner plans with our friends. "Wanna go shower and get ready to go out? Maybe we could do something radical and discuss baby names while I wash your hair, or is that pushing it too far?"

"Actually . . . " She stroked her fingertips down my cheek. "I have two names in mind. It's funny. I walked downstairs this morning, and they just came to me. Now I can't get them out of my head."

"So?" I held my breath. "What are they?"

As Gemma told me the names, one boy's and one girl's, water welled in my eyes. I'd wanted to come up with names along the same lines, using the same theme, but I'd failed. She'd nailed it. "I love them. They're perfect."

I helped Gemma to her feet and led her into our bedroom. As we fell under the warmth of the cascading water, I planted soft kisses against her lips.

With a heartwarming smile, I whispered, "I wonder which one it will be? A boy or a girl?"

We'd find out soon enough.
I couldn't wait to meet our child.
Only four weeks to go.

Chapter 15

KARA

Backstage at Spring Studios, preparing for Ivory Mink's September fashion show, I zipped the stunning curvy model, Isla, into her black silky, flowing dress. My heart thudded against my ribs. I'd been to many Fashion Week events before, but this was the first time I'd designed gowns for the show, not worked on someone else's vision. Even better than that, the dresses held my name, not Ivory's. The Kara Collins Limited Collection was about to be revealed to the world. My fingers trembled as I tied the long halter-neck sashes into a bow. My stomach churned like it had on the first day of school. It was a dream come true to see my couture on the catwalk.

Throughout the overcrowded dressing room, an electric buzz hovered in the air. Models sat in front of vanity mirrors getting final touches by makeup artists and hairstylists. Assistants darted in and around the chairs and tables, grabbing last-minute accessories for outfits. The production crew kept making sure we were on schedule. Security hovered near the doorways. Clothes racks overloaded with gowns covered in sequins, ostrich feathers, and rhinestones lined the walls. Stiletto shoes lay scattered on the floor beneath them.

I drew in a deep breath to find some calm in the chaos. To stay focused. But the noise and commotion in the room didn't help.

Ivory clipped a diamond choker around Isla's neck. "There. You're done. Go line up, please." Ivory pointed to the row of girls set to strut down the catwalk.

"You ready?" Ivory Mink flicked her hot pink braids over her shoulder and hugged me tight. "This never gets old." Her energy level would rock the Richter scale off the charts. "This is my seventh show, but every time feels like the first."

"Your gowns are amazing." I opened another jewelry box on the table to complete the next model's outfit. "Gem's already picked out two of your outfits. The teal sequined playsuit and the red cocktail dress."

"Oh, yay." Ivory clapped her hands. "I love dressing her. She rocks. Thank you for introducing us." She rubbed my arm. "I can't thank you enough. I count my lucky stars every day that, out of all the fashion houses in New York, you picked mine to work with. We were meant to find each other."

What? Ivory was thankful for me? It was the other way around. I had found a niche within Ivory's fashion house to design outfits for elite customers like Gemma, some of my friends, and old clients like Elise, who I'd worked for at Conrad's Fashion House. "No. Thank you for the opportunity to design again. I wish I could work full-time, but I love styling for Everhide too much."

"Girlfriend." Ivory clicked her fingers. "We are modern women in a modern world. We're both moms with kids and mighty fine husbands. I'm all about flexibility, sister. We deserve to have it all."

Yes, we did.

Everything had fallen into place. After some setbacks, and surviving several heartbreaking hurdles, I'd found my stride. I had not one, but two incredible jobs, a gorgeous daughter, twins on the way, and the hottest, most supportive husband in the world. I'd never been this happy.

The next model stepped in front of me.

Ivory gave me another quick hug. "I love you. But I've gotta rush. It's nearly showtime, and I have two models to dress."

"Okay." I wiped my clammy hands on my dress pants. "Let me know if you need a hand."

"Will do. See you soon." Ivory disappeared into the sea of people preparing for the show.

Refocusing, I turned to my model. "Rita, this is stunning on you." I straightened the shoulders of the gown. The flowing pale pink organza minidress, covered in tiny crystals, with long sheer sleeves, caught the light every time Rita moved.

"It feels amazing." Rita ran her hand over the empire-line bodice.

"And you look like a goddess in it," I said. Rita was a six-foot-one, African American beauty; she'd look good in a recycled shopping bag. I grabbed the crystal-encrusted headband out of the jewelry box and placed it on Rita's head. "Perfect. Now go. Go. Go."

After prepping my last model, I glanced at my watch. Ten minutes to go.

A murmur rippled through the crowd. People's gazes diverted toward the entrance. I turned to see what was happening. Hunter strode toward me in a sexy-as-hell charcoal dinner suit, carrying our daughter. *What a sight!* My heart fluttered like a firefly. Ashleigh wriggled in his arms, wanting to be put down, but he hugged her close and tickled her tummy. Behind him were Gemma and Kyle. Diego and security stayed by the door.

But why was Gemma here? She was due and about to pop at any moment.

"Hey." Hunter kissed me hello. "You set?"

My hands shook as I fidgeted with my strand of pearls. "I think so."

Ashleigh held out her tiny hand toward me. "Ma. Ma. Ma."

"Hey sweetie." I stepped forward and kissed her cheek. "Stay with Daddy. I'll see you real soon."

"We came to wish you luck." Gemma held her arms wide.

"I love you for coming." I bent my knees to hug Gemma, then clutched her hand. "But you shouldn't be here."

"I'm okay." Gemma feigned a smile. No sparkle touched her eyes. "I wouldn't miss your show for the world."

"Can't keep her down." Kyle straightened his tie, then gave me a kiss on the cheek. "Love your dresses, Kar. Congratulations."

"It's so exciting." Jitters skipped through my voice. I flattened my hand against my stomach to ease the mounting nerves. "Is Lexi ready?"

"Yeah." Hunter jerked his head toward the showroom door. "She's out front, ready to take photos. Hayds is playing assistant."

"Awesome." I nodded.

"Five minutes." The production manager held up his hand, hollering from the side of the stage.

Oh, crap. The show would be livestreamed across the globe. Anna Wintour sat in the front row alongside other fashion magazine editors from *Harper's Bazaar*, *InStyle* and *Elle*. Jennifer Anniston, Emma Stone, and Cardi B were among the long list of celebrities, leading stylists, and influencers in the audience. My head throbbed and spun. I didn't know how my friends could perform in front of thousands of fans without the nerves rendering them useless. I wasn't even on stage, and I felt like passing out.

Hunter stepped in front of me with Ashleigh sitting on his hip. He caressed the back of my head and drew me forward so our foreheads touched. "Breathe."

Hmm. I closed my eyes and inhaled the scent of his Dior cologne. Citrusy. Alluring. Sensual. Absorbing him into every cell in my body calmed me more than meditation.

He smoothed his hand over the back of my hair. "The dresses are fab. The stage looks amazing. The models are set. So now, enjoy the show and have fun." He gave me a quick kiss. "I love you."

"Thank you." I wiped the smudge of my lipstick off his lips, then kissed Ashleigh. "Love you, too."

Ashleigh grabbed a handful of my hair and pulled. "Mama."

Ow! I winced as I untangled my hair from Ashleigh's tiny fingers and kissed them. "Stay with Daddy." Maybe we should've left Ashleigh at home with Diego, but he'd wanted to see the show.

"Be good, and I'll see you soon."

God, I loved my family.

"Whoa!" Gemma clutched her belly and seized Kyle's arm. The color drained from her face.

"Gem?" My breath snagged in my throat. "Are you okay?"

"Yep. Yep. I'm fine." Fear darkened her eyes as she rubbed her abdomen. "Don't worry about me."

"Babe?" Kyle circled his hand over her back. "Are you sure? Our driver is waiting downstairs, ready to get us out of here if needed."

"No." Gemma sucked in a deep breath and let it out slowly. "It's nothing. I'm not missing Kara's first showing." But she jolted forward, clutching her baby bump. "Arrrrgh. Fuck!"

"Two minutes," the stage manager's voice boomed across the room of gathered models and crew.

Shit. I glanced at the girls rushing to the side of the stage and shuffling into position. "Gem. I've gotta go." My heart pounded. I pointed at Gemma's baby bump. "Stay. Wait half an hour and this will all be over. Then, you can come."

"Um . . ." Gemma closed her eyes and swayed on her feet. "Ooooh." Sweat broke out on her brow. "Shit. Shit. Shit."

Worry washed across Hunter's face. "Gem, you're in labor." Ashleigh cried and squirmed. Hunter grabbed a sparkly gold bangle off the table and gave it to her to play with—anything to distract her and stop her from wriggling around like a monkey. "You need to go to the hospital."

Gemma closed her eyes and shook her head. "No-pe. I can't be. No. No. Not yet."

"Ahh . . . yeah." Kyle's eyes widened, terror and excitement flickered in their depths. "Are the pains getting worse?"

"No . . . yes . . . maybe. It can wait." Gemma clutched her lower back. "I've had them all morning. It's nothing."

"All morning?" I spluttered. It was now nearly three p.m. "Gemma. It's baby time. Don't just stand there. Go." I caught Gemma's shoulders, turned her toward the door, and marched her forward. "You crazy woman. Go have your baby."

But Gemma took a few steps and stopped. She swung around to face me. "No. Your show."

I wanted to hug and hold Gemma so tight. Gemma's support and selflessness were beyond words, but her baby took precedence. "You can watch the video later. Go. I'll come to the hospital as soon as I can." After the show, there was an after-party where I would have to mingle with the guests, journalists, and influencers. I wouldn't be out of there until ten p.m. or later. Gemma might have had her baby by then. *So exciting.* I wrapped my arms around Gemma's shoulders and squeezed her close. "I love you. But go. Take the drugs. Good luck."

"I'm scared," Gemma whispered. A tear slid down her cheek.

"I know. But you're strong and resilient. Go get that baby out of you."

"I'm sorry." Her chin quivered.

"Don't be silly. Go."

I stepped back. Hunter's gaze lingered on Gemma, no doubt torn between staying by my side and wanting to be with his friend. He dashed forward with Ashleigh on his hip, embraced Gemma, and kissed her on top of the head. "Go. Scream the house down. I wanna hear you curse all the way across Manhattan." He ruffled her hair. "Love you."

He hugged and slapped Kyle on the back. "Good luck, bud."

"Thanks, man." Kyle grabbed Gemma's hand, and they headed for the door. Swiping his hand from side to side, he hollered at the group of makeup artists and hairstylists blocking the way, ogling him and Hunter. "Move, please. The baby's coming. Quick. Get out of the way. Gem's in labor. MOVE."

I stifled my laugh, biting my lip hard. I'd never seen Kyle so demanding.

Sam, head of Everhide's security, charged forward, clearing the path for them. He opened the side door, and Kyle and Gemma disappeared outside.

My heartbeat thundered like a thousand galloping horses. I wiped a tear from my eye. "Holy shit. Gem's about to have her baby."

"That's totally fucking surreal." Hunter's gaze remained locked on the door.

"Hey?" I touched his arm. "She'll be okay."

"I know." He nodded, but his voice lacked conviction. "It's weird not being with her for such a huge occasion. But this . . ." He turned to me, smiled, and drew me close to kiss my lips. "This is your big occasion and just as important. Gem has Kyle, and I have you. Here, with my gorgeous wife, and our beautiful daughter, is where I want to be. Always."

I ran my fingertips down his chiseled cheekbone. Gemma having a baby was a much bigger deal than my show, but I loved him for staying. He always chose me now. He put Ashleigh and me before music, before Kyle and Gemma. I had never felt so loved, adored, and cherished. So content, blessed, and happy. Hunter was my one. The true love of my life.

Ashleigh flicked the bangle she'd been playing with and hit Hunter in the chin. "Ow! You little—" He groaned, grabbed her tiny hand, and kissed it. "Good thing you're cute." He handed the bangle to me, complete with baby slobber. Ashleigh's bottom lip hit the ground, but she didn't protest. "We'll go take our seats before she does some serious damage to my face. Knock 'em dead, Pearl. You and Ivory will be the talk of the town tomorrow."

I clutched the bangle to my chest and giggled. "No, I think Gem will take the headlines."

"And you'll be right up there with her. Love you. Go break a leg." Hunter kissed my cheek again, turned on his heels, and wove through the maze of people with Ashleigh in his arms. Diego joined him, and they headed out into the main event area.

As the door closed behind them, the lights dimmed.

Shit. Showtime.

I wiped the bangle clean on a nearby towel, dropped it on the table, and ran over to the line of models.

Standing beside Ivory, I did one last check of the first model's outfit. *Straps are good. Skirt straight. Zip zipped. All set.*

My mind spiraled and swirled. *Wow.* Gemma was in labor. My first show was about to start.

The *dah-dah-dadada-dah* electric beat of Kylie Minogue's "Can't Get Blue Monday Out of My Head" reverberated through the speakers. Lights flashed, flickered, and swirled across the stage. Smoke billowed from the fog machine and snaked across the catwalk.

My heart pounded in time with the super-fast disco beat. This was my moment. The models were ready. The clothes looked spectacular.

"Was that Gemma leaving?" Ivory re-tied the belt sash on her model's dress and puffed out the bow. "Is everything okay?"

"Yeah." My voice shook as much as my nerves. "She just went into labor."

"Holy crap."

"She'll be fine." I prayed so. After my traumatic baby history, I wouldn't stop worrying until I knew Gemma and the baby were all right. I wouldn't relax. At least the show was a temporary distraction. I buckled on a brilliant smile and pushed my anxiety aside. "Let's rock this place."

The first model climbed the five steps onto the stage. She strode over to the center spotlight, struck a pose, smiled, and headed down the catwalk.

I closed my eyes. I pinned this moment in my memory bank. *I did it. My first gown is on the runway. A dream come true.*

But I also said a silent prayer for Gemma and the baby. *Please. Please. Please. Be okay.*

Chapter 16

GEMMA

"Fuuuuck!" I clutched my belly, curled onto my side, and ignored the nurse checking my vitals—temperature, heart rate, blood pressure. The monitoring pads stuck to my stomach tweaked and pulled. Screens blazed beside my bed, and equipment blipped and buzzed around me. Kyle stood beside me, clutching my hand and stroking my hair. His soothing touch was cool against my burning forehead, but it did nothing to relieve the painful contractions.

I'd been here for three hours.

I wanted this baby out . . . *now!*

Midwife Melanie's brow furrowed as she pulled off the cuff from my arm after taking my blood pressure. "Gemma?" Melanie reached across the bed and pressed the call button. "I'm just going to get the doctor."

"Why?" Wooziness whirled through my head. "What's wrong? Is the baby okay?"

"Everything's fine." She placed her hand on my arm. "Your blood pressure is a touch on the high side."

"What does that mean?" Worry flooded Kyle's eyes.

"Of course it's fucking high," I groaned. "I'm having a fucking baby."

"Let's wait and see what the doctor suggests." Melanie gave

me a quick smile and dashed out of the room.

I squeezed Kyle's hand to ground myself. "Kyle?"

"I'm sure it's nothing." He kissed my fingers. "The nurse just needs to make sure you and the baby are okay."

Kyle couldn't mask the fear in his tone.

Panic slid through my veins. I'd had enough hospital emergencies to last a lifetime—I didn't need another.

Two minutes later, my doctor entered the room with the nurse. "Hey, Gemma? How are you feeling?"

"How the hell do you think I am? I'm in labor. I'm missing my friend's first fashion show. This thing won't come out. And it hurts."

"Yep." Dr. Singh gave me a warm smile, grabbed my medical chart, and scanned the monitors. "I've had two children without pain relief. I know what you're going through."

Dr. Singh was always direct and to the point. She didn't sugarcoat anything. I liked her a lot. I'd love her even more if she stopped the pain.

Dr. Singh straightened her glasses and glanced at the monitors, reread my chart, then checked the monitors again. She reached for a pair of rubber gloves out of the box hanging on the wall. "Gemma, I need to check if you've dilated any further."

I groaned and rolled onto my back. "Do you enjoy looking up vaginas?"

"Yes, because I love delivering babies." Dr. Singh snapped on the gloves and wriggled her fingers. "Bringing life into the world is very rewarding. Ready?"

I screwed up my nose and clutched at the bedsheet as the doctor examined me. *So. Not. Pleasant.*

As the doctor disposed of her gloves, my belly lurched. My eyes watered as I clutched my baby bump. "Arrrrgh. Why does it have to hurt?"

"It will all be worth it in the end," the midwife said, but her eyes remained glued to the baby monitor.

"You're doing great, Gem." Kyle placed a cool cloth on my

forehead. He was much calmer than I'd expected. Forever my rock, my steady hand in times of need.

"I will gladly trade places with you." My voice slid through my clenched teeth, then I turned my attention to the doctor. "When can I have the drugs?" I wanted pain relief. I wanted it now.

"Just give me a sec." The doctor stepped in front of the monitor, watched the blips and lines zigzagging across the screen for a few seconds, then turned to me. "Gemma, your contractions are five minutes apart, but you're not dilated at all. Your blood pressure is bordering on too high, and the baby's heartbeat is faster than we'd like to see."

"So, what do we do?" Kyle's hand sweated in my grip.

"There are two options. Option one is we give you some pain relief, monitor you closely for a while longer, maybe twenty minutes to half an hour, and see if things settle. Option two is a cesarean. If your blood pressure doesn't come down, we don't want you pushing the baby out or the baby getting more distressed."

Distressed? "What do you think is best?" I didn't care if I didn't have a natural birth. A C-section would get this over and done with. I'd been prepared for anything, and I was happy to go with the flow. My tummy cinched. I pressed my palm against the pain pummeling my lower abdomen, and a tear slid from my eye. "Argh. This thing is gonna kill me."

"Gemma?" The doctor's gaze stayed pinned to the baby monitor, the heart rate digits slowly rising. "You need to relax."

"Relax? Are you fucking with me?"

"Come on, Gem." Kyle rubbed and patted my hand. "Breathe with me."

Fuck breathing. I wanted this thing out.

The monitor's alarm pierced the air.

Red lights flashed across the screen.

"What's happening?" I tried to sit up, but my belly ached too much.

"It's okay." The doctor's smile was calm and collected, but a sense of urgency strained her voice. "The baby is fine. So are you. We have these alarms set to give us plenty of time. But you just selected option two. Well, your little one did. We're going to take you to an operating room straight away for an emergency cesarean. It's best for you and the baby."

"Okay." My head sank into the pillow, but I trembled all over. "Just do what you have to do." I hadn't carried this damn baby for nine months for something to go wrong now. I'd be having stern words with this kid when it arrived. *Do not stress me out!*

"Gem?"

Kyle's whisper snagged my heart. The fear in his eyes made me sick to the stomach. The dread in his tone tore at my soul. We'd been through enough drama in our lives—we didn't need anymore. But an operation meant risk.

He smoothed his hand over my hair. "I'll be right by your side every step of the way."

Tears pricked the backs of my eyes as I nodded. "I know."

This was a level of anxiety I hadn't anticipated. I'd been in danger before—I'd come close to dying. But now our baby's life was under threat. I didn't want anything to go wrong. Not with our baby. Why couldn't we get a break?

"I'll make a quick call." Dr. Singh finished writing on her chart, then handed the folder to the nurse. "Gemma, please give me a few minutes, and I'll find out which operating room we can use."

The doctor rushed out of the room. The midwife stayed, monitoring the screens.

I rolled onto my side to face Kyle, shuffled backward and tugged him forward. "Lie with me."

He rolled up the long sleeves of his button-down shirt, then stretched out on the bed beside me. He'd discarded his dinner jacket and tie earlier. They lay draped over the nearby chair. He swiped my hair off my face, tucked it behind my ear, and kissed my lips.

Even when I was scared and uncertain, and the unknown lay ahead, I never forgot to appreciate how good life was. I never forgot how much I loved him. I brushed my fingertip across his fine, straight eyebrows and down the smooth slope of his jaw. My fingers shook as I traced the curve of his lips and dragged my thumb over the scar on his chin that I'd given him years ago, accidentally hitting him with my guitar. I memorized every gorgeous feature of his face for the millionth time. The scent of his spicy cologne soothed my troubled mind. One glance into his eyes connected our souls. He was my life, my love—my everything. But in a short while, life would never be the same. Our music. Our home. Our world. We'd be three, not two.

Why the hell did I ever agree to this?

I laugh-cried over my tears and kissed his lips. "I love you."

He breathed me in. "More than my own life."

That was why we were having a baby.

I loved him more than my own life.

The orderly arrived and Kyle jumped off the bed. I didn't want to let go of him. My heart rate quickened as the orderly unplugged my bed at pace, raised the side rails, and wheeled me out of the room.

Was the situation more dire than the doctor had let on?

Inside the operating room, four nurses helped slide me over onto the procedure table. They jostled around me, moving trolleys of implements into position, reattaching me to a plethora of monitors and machines, and placing a surgical cap on my head. I shivered all over, clutching at my aching belly. I didn't know if my chills were from the freezing air-conditioning or from the fear forming icicles in my veins. No doubt . . . both.

"Where's Kyle?" My teeth chattered as a nurse placed a warm blanket over me.

"I'm here." He rushed to my side, dressed in disposable blue scrubs over his suit pants and button-down shirt, and a surgical cap covering his hair. "You okay?"

"No. My head's woozy." The stench of sanitizer overpowering the room didn't help. "And I'm c-c-cold."

He sat on the stool beside me, caught my hand between his palms, and drew it toward his mouth. He kissed my knuckles, then blew his warm breath onto my fingertips and rubbed them. "That better?"

"Yeah."

"Gemma?" Dr. Singh, fully garbed in scrubs, came to my side. "We're ready to start. This is Dr. Thompson, the anesthetist." She jutted her chin toward the man on the opposite side of the bed. "He'll insert an epidural into your back. Within a minute or two, you won't feel a thing, and we'll get your baby out."

"Is it still okay?" I asked, my anxiety coiling higher and higher.

"Yes, Gemma." Dr. Singh rubbed my arm.

"If something happens, you save the baby. Not me."

Where did that come from?

"Gemma." Dr. Singh's eyes twinkled over her mask, but seriousness set in her tone. "I haven't lost anyone yet, mother or child. And I'm not about to start. You're fit, healthy, and so is the baby. Shall we begin?"

My heart barreled up to my throat. My mouth ran dry. Each breath was a short pant. I closed my eyes and nodded.

"Hi Gemma, I'm Brendan." Dr. Thompson peered over his face mask. Silver hair peeked out from beneath his cap. His eyes glinted like George Clooney's. "I need you to roll onto your side toward Kyle, please? Curl into a ball. I'll give you a local anesthetic, then insert the epidural. Okay?"

As the doctor gave me the needle, a sting exploded across my skin and cold liquid entered my back. I squeezed Kyle's hand so tight his knuckles turned white. He winced, leaned forward and kissed me but didn't ask me to release my grip.

Thirty seconds later, there was a wriggle and a prod of something low in my back, but no pain.

I tried to focus on Kyle, but stars flickered before my eyes. "Kyle . . . I'm scared."

"Me too." He stroked my forehead and held my hand. "It will be over soon. You ready to meet our baby?"

"No." I shut my eyes. I didn't want to think about being sliced open with a scalpel.

"Gemma, we need you to roll onto your back now," Dr. Singh said, holding up her latex-gloved hands.

Why couldn't I move? Why were my legs all tingly? I couldn't feel my toes. Or my baby. Panic strangled my throat.

Two nurses helped turn me, then erected a blue sheet across my chest.

My heart pounded like a hammer in my throat, my head, and my chest. My body shivered and shook. "Kyle? Why am I shaking?" Tears prickled my eyes. "What's wrong?"

An oxygen mask was placed over my face. Darkness tunneled my vision. Fear laced every inch of my body.

"What's happening?" Kyle asked the nurse monitoring the screens.

"She's okay," the nurse said. "But we've got to get the baby out."

The baby? What was wrong with the baby?

"Can you feel this, Gemma?" Dr. Singh asked.

"Feel what?" Dizziness swam through my head.

"That's a good thing."

Was Dr. Singh hovering over my belly?

Oh, God. I wanted to be sick. My head swayed from side to side.

"Gem?" Kyle's voice cracked. "What are you doing?"

My eyes rolled shut. Fever flushed my skin.

"Gem?" Panic rippled through Kyle's tone. "Stay with me. Gem? You're okay, baby. You're okay."

What was beeping? Why couldn't I open my eyes? What was happening?

There was a tug and a pull in my lower body.

A deep whooshing sound filled my head. My hearing turned fuzzy, like my ears were blocked.

No. No. Fight. *Fight.*

My vision blurred. I couldn't see anything. Feel anything.

Kyle? Kyle? KYLE?

The world spun. My heartbeat stampeded against my ribs.

Shit. What's happening?

Then . . . nothing. The darkness had claimed me.

***

I blinked my eyes open. It took me a couple of seconds to focus. A nurse hovered over me. I was still in the operating room. Other surgical staff lingered around my lower body, and over by the side of the room.

Crying? Was that crying?

"There you are." The nurse's kind blue eyes sparkled as if she were smiling behind her mask. "You're okay. You fainted. That's all."

Fainted?

"Hey, precious." Kyle's eyes glistened with tears as he leaned over and kissed my forehead. "You scared me half to death."

"Sorry," I whispered.

"Guess what?" He stroked my hair.

"What?"

"We have a daughter."

My heart dipped and soared. A tear slid down my cheek. "A daughter?"

"Hey Gemma." Dr. Singh came over and placed the tiny sleepy baby, wrapped in a soft, striped blanket on my chest. "Delivered as promised. Her heart is fine. There were no other issues. She was just eager to meet you."

I cradled my baby and sobbed. "Oh my God. We have a baby girl." With tender strokes, I traced the curve of her nose, skimmed the line of her chin, and touched her pale pink lips. *Oh, wow!* She was a mini-Kyle. But the soft dark hair covering her head and the curve of her eyebrows were like mine.

"All fingers and toes accounted for." Kyle caressed her head. "Lungs are definitely in working order. You missed her crying when she came out. I think she's exhausted now."

So was I.

But as I pressed my lips against her forehead, the world distorted. My center of gravity altered. My heartbeat rocked and reset to a new rhythm—all for my daughter. "She's perfect."

Teary-eyed, Kyle nodded and sniffled. "You both are. You did good, Gem."

After a nurse took several photos for us, I glanced at Kyle. "So? Do you think the name we chose suits her?"

"Absolutely."

Our baby licked her lips, her brow furrowed, but she stayed sleeping. I drew her closer and smiled, still amazed she was finally in my arms. I whispered, "Hello, Skye."

We'd picked the name because the sky had no limits. We'd promised to give our child every opportunity imaginable and to let her chase her dreams. Because that was what we'd done every day since we'd met.

Kyle wiped the dampness from his eyes. "I can't believe she's here. We have our little Skye. I'm so proud of you, Gem." The baby wriggled against my chest. "Just promise me one thing."

"What's that?"

"Please don't scare the living crap out of me ever again. I thought I'd lost you."

The agony in his voice tore my heart. I never wanted to hurt him.

"Okay." I nodded as a tear slid down my cheek. "I'll try not to."

Dr. Singh touched my shoulder. "If you're ready, we'll take you back to the ward now."

I flicked away my tears with my fingertips and wiped them on my gown. "Okay."

As Kyle held onto the edge of the bed and I held Skye in my arms, the orderly wheeled me back to our room.

I couldn't take my eyes off Skye. The universe had thrown me another curveball; one I'd never expected. Like it had done on the day I'd walked into high school and met two gangling teenage boys. Like on the day I'd played music with Kyle and Hunter for the first time. Like on the day we'd signed with SureHaven all those years ago. Many events had impacted my life, but falling in love and marrying my best friend, my soul mate, had topped the list as the best. Now, us having a child was on par. I was determined to turn that tiny mistake nine months ago into the best decision of my life.

Placing my hand on Skye's heart, I whispered, "I promise I am gonna love the shit out of you. You have done something to me. I don't know what it is. But I swear. I'm never, ever, gonna let you go."

With Kyle by my side, my daughter in my arms, I headed toward my new life. As a rockstar. As a wife. As a mom.

Nothing would hold me back.

Chapter 17

Declan Andrew Moore was born on November 7th at 3:23 p.m., right on his due date. After struggling to get him to feed and a restless night of broken sleep, I lay stretched out on the hospital bed. It was mid-morning. Exhaustion had seeped like leaden liquid into my bones. I winced as Declan suckled my sore, aching breast. My nipples stung. I needed a shower. My eyelashes weighed a ton. Crying was imminent.

Hayden leaned over me and kissed my brow. Shadows circled his eyes. His *I'm-so-fucking-tired* smile reflected my fatigue.

Yep. Good. He can suffer too. *We're in this parenting thing together.*

But underneath the tiredness, the unrelenting happiness shimmering in the depths of Hayden's eyes made having Declan worth it.

"He's so tiny," Hayden whispered, peering down at Declan.

"My vagina has a different opinion about that."

"Angel, I don't know how you did it. Thank fuck I never have to go through childbirth."

My head sank into the pillow, and I found a smidgen of strength to smile. Every time I'd screamed during the birth, Hayden had cringed and clutched his stomach. He'd groaned and grunted as if feeling every one of my contractions and pushes. He'd stressed, hyperventilated and passed out. My big, tough drummer. *Not!*

There was a knock at the door.

"Come in." Hayden hollered.

In strode our friends.

I closed my eyes, and a tear caught on my eyelashes. I was so happy to see them but was spent of all my energy. Thank goodness they'd only be here for a quick visit.

Kara carried Ashleigh and a huge fluffy white teddy bear in her arms. Hunter brought in a huge bunch of blue and white balloons and flowers. Gemma held more flowers and a tiger plush toy. Kyle cradled Skye in his arms.

"Hi." Gemma eased over to the bed and kissed my cheek, then rushed around the bed to hug Hayden, shoving the toy into his chest. Her figure had trimmed down after having Skye. Her energy was as vibrant as a pride parade. There was nothing in Gemma's appearance that suggested she'd had a baby two months ago. "Congratulations."

God, I hope my figure bounces back like that.

"Hey Lex." Kara came over to the bed, cupped Declan's head and straightened his pale blue beanie. "Ohhhh . . . look at your little man. He's gorgeous."

"He takes after his mommy." I swooned as I held Declan's hand against my chest while he fed. He had fair skin and fine blond hair like me. His nose and lips were the same shape as mine too. At a stretch, he had Hayden's chin, but that was where the resemblance stopped.

"Sorry we're visiting so early, but we're on our way to lunch." Hunter placed the flowers on the nightstand.

"We didn't plan this release well, did we?" I sighed as I eased Declan off one boob and attached him to the other. Now he'd gotten the hang of drinking, he didn't want to stop. "I can't believe I worked for over a year on this project and I'm missing the celebrations."

I wasn't upset, but I pulled out my finest pout anyway.

After the success of Everhide's first documentary, which covered their rise from a high school band to the recording of their sixth studio album, they'd signed an agreement last year to release their fifth world tour concert, *Kiss This*, on Netflix. The film's date had been set before I'd gotten pregnant and couldn't be altered with everyone's busy Christmas calendars. Even if I could go, I'd probably fall asleep during the appetizers.

"Don't be silly." Kyle gently rocked and swayed a sleeping Skye in his arms. "Declan is way more important. We'll celebrate with you when you're home."

"I'm gonna hold you to that." I waggled my finger at Kyle. "It better involve Bollinger." But I'd be breastfeeding. No alcohol. *Damn it.*

He chuckled and nodded. "Anything you want, it's yours."

I'd worked on so many other projects that had blown my mind—I couldn't be upset about missing one launch. I couldn't thank my friends enough for giving me the most incredible opportunities. Every day I got to do what I loved—taking photographs, managing their social media, designing artwork and executing marketing campaigns. Working with Kate, their publicist, and Clinton, their creative director, had taken my dreams and aspirations to a whole new level. I'd been so fortunate to have met such an amazing bunch of people. Gemma, Hunter, and Kyle loved me like family. I'd always wished upon the stars; I'd never imagined I'd end up working for three of the brightest ones.

Hayden leaned against the bed next to me and faced his bandmates. "Are you taking Skye to the lunch?"

"Yeah." Gemma wrapped her arm around Kyle's waist and rested her head against his shoulder. "It's her first official outing. She has to get used to this lifestyle, being our kid. I'll go to the lunch for a while, then head home with Diego and Ashleigh. Kyle, Hunt, and Kar can stay, schmoozing the execs."

"Oh," I threw her a cheeky grin. "Are you doing that motherhood thing?"

"I know." Gemma wrinkled her nose. "It's so weird, right?"

"It's not weird, Gem." Kara sat Ashleigh on the end of the bed and straightened her daughter's cute little Burberry dress. Kara tilted her head toward Gemma. "You're awesome with Skye. You should still take it easy."

"I feel fine. Not breastfeeding helps." Gemma shimmied her shoulders and clutched her boobs. "Glad these little puppies didn't produce milk."

I gazed down at Declan. Maybe Gemma was onto something if feeding kept hurting like this. I was in utter agony.

Ashleigh squealed as she clung onto the teddy bear. But Kara stopped her from chewing on its fluffy ears. "Sorry, the bear might have some bonus dribble."

At nearly seventeen months old, Ashleigh had grown into the most adorable toddler—a spitting image of her daddy. She was destined to break many hearts when she grew up.

"It's fine, Kar. We'll have to get used to baby slobber." I covered my boobs and handed Declan to Hayden for burping.

"Can I burp him?" Kara's eyes brightened, and she held out her hands. "I need practice for the twins next month."

There was way too much excitement in Kara's voice. Would she be this vibrant after a couple of weeks of juggling twins? *Yeah . . . probably.*

"He's all yours." Hayden walked around the end of the bed and handed Declan to Kara. Hunter stepped in to mind Ashleigh.

"So?" Kara jutted her chin toward me as she rocked Declan on her shoulder and patted his tiny back. "How was it? The birth? Was it all okay?"

"No." I smoothed my hands over my now floppy belly. "It was awful. Seven hours of labor. I tore. I've had stitches. Hayden vomited and passed out."

"You what?" Hunter laughed. "You vomited?"

"Yeah." Hayden ruffled his fingers through his hair. "Not my finest moment. But there was all this goo and gunk. It was horrible and gross."

I caught his hand and smiled at him. He often threw up before big concerts. Nerves had always gotten the better of him—I guessed blood did too. "But a nurse was very quick to rush to your rescue."

A little too quick for my liking, but I'd had other things to worry about . . . like giving birth.

Hayden placed his hand over his chest and mocked shock. "I could've been hurt."

"You're such a pussy." Kyle chuckled, patting Skye's bottom while she slept.

"Yep." Hayden didn't deny it. "Lucky Lex loves me."

"Yeah." I entwined our fingers and kissed his hand. "I do."

After more jokes and hugs, cuddles, and photos with Declan, our friends headed off to the launch. As the door clicked closed behind them, peace settled across the room. Silence had never sounded so good. As Declan snuggled against my chest, I sank lower in the bed. "Hayds, I'm sorry you're missing the lunch."

"I'm not." He swept one of my curls off my forehead. "There is nowhere I'd rather be than here with you. There will be countless opportunities for promos and launches and tours in the future. More videos. More shoots. More music. But there was only one chance to see our baby born. I wouldn't have missed that for the world."

He was right. It had been a momentous occasion.

Our careers would only get better and better. With two singles released this year, and another due to drop in January before they worked on the new album, the spotlight was ready and waiting for more Everhide. Hayden had blended seamlessly into the band. And I was there capturing every moment.

"Thank you for being here." I cupped his cheek. "I wouldn't have made it through without you."

"Yeah, I'm pretty sure you would have."

"True." My eyes fluttered closed. *God. I'm tired.*

Hayden chuckled, stroked my hair and kissed my lips. He took Declan from my arms. "Angel, get some sleep. We won't have long before he wakes for another feed."

"Okay." I wouldn't argue. I pulled the blankets over my chest and tugged the pillow beneath my head. The bed was hard and uncomfortable, but right then, it was heaven.

"I love you." He placed a soft kiss on my brow, then slipped onto the recliner by the window with Declan sleeping against his shoulder. Undeniable contentment lit Hayden's face as he sang softly and covered Declan in a blanket.

I wanted to listen to his lyrics. I'd never heard them before. But my body had other ideas. My eyelids grew heavier and heavier. Within seconds, I drifted off to sleep.

***

Four days after Declan was born, I headed home from the hospital. But Hayden didn't take me and our baby to our old apartment in the West Village. Instead, we headed to our new condo in Tribeca. After a few delays with the previous owner's relocation to Dubai, we'd finally bought the place next to Kyle and Gemma's. No other condo had come close to being suitable.

My stomach somersaulted more than a Cirque du Soleil performer. It was our first night in our new home. Our first night without a nurse to help with Declan. Our first night as a new family.

Hayden held Declan in the baby carrier in one hand and opened the door with the other.

Dragging my overnight bag behind me, I wove around them and stepped inside the foyer. The overpowering smell of fresh paint and new furniture filled the air. As I walked into the living area, my heart thudded and my eyes watered. I dumped my bag and purse by the kitchen island. Placing my hands on top of the counter, I took a deep breath to steady myself.

This is home. Our home.

I'd been here several times over the past week, moving our belongings over from our old apartment, putting away items, and styling the rooms with a few new pieces of furniture. But it was still hard to comprehend that this was ours.

Hayden placed the baby carrier on the island and lifted Declan out. He eased over to stand beside me with our baby nestled in his arms. Declan was sound asleep, oblivious to his surroundings.

I hooked my arm around Hayden's back and rested my head against his shoulder. "I can't believe this is our home."

"Yeah." Hayden kissed me on the temple. "It's like a dream, isn't it?"

"I'm afraid I'm going to wake up, and it will all disappear."

"I assure you; this is no dream." He caressed Declan's tiny head. "It's mind-blowing that everything we hoped to achieve has become our reality."

"We did it, didn't we?" A lone tear zigzagged down my cheek. "Our New York dreams have come true. But this little one is certainly a bonus." I leaned forward and kissed Declan's head. "We have a beautiful baby."

Since I'd met Hayden in college, our lives had evolved into something beyond my expectations. We'd gone from friends to lovers to becoming a family.

Declan wriggled in Hayden's arms. A cry burst from his tiny lungs. Hayden swayed gently, bouncing and rocking Declan from side to side. "It's okay. Shh."

"He probably needs a diaper change . . . and a feed." I winced, rubbing at the tendrils of pain shooting through the top of my breasts. The second Declan cried, my milk came down. It ached. It hurt. I needed relief, if nothing else.

"You get ready to feed him." Hayden swooped in to steal a kiss from my lips. "I'll change his pants." As he stepped backward toward the bedrooms, he whispered, "I love you."

"Same." I blew him a kiss. "But before Declan disturbs everyone in the building, we better get him fed."

"I'll be right back."

As Hayden disappeared down the hallway, I grabbed my water bottle and a cloth out of the diaper bag and settled onto our new sofa. Hayden returned and handed me Declan. Dressed in a navy-striped onesie, Declan was as light as a cloud, tiny and perfect in every way.

As I fed Declan, Hayden sat beside me, stroking my hair. His gaze set on my face.

"What?" I whispered.

"You're just so beautiful." He tucked one of my wayward curls behind my ear. "Our new home is incredible. But I will always be grateful that I get to wake up next to you every day. We get to do what we love every day. We have a son. But none of this would've been possible or meant anything if I didn't have you by my side. You're my life, Lex. My angel."

I smiled and let my head fall back against the soft headrest. My heart overflowed with love. "We've taken some crazy, windy roads to get here, haven't we?"

"We sure have." His eyes glinted, but our past lingered in their depths. "But now I just want to take care of you and Declan and make you happy for the rest of my days."

I leaned over and pressed my lips against his. Declan kept drinking. "Hayds, this is my happily ever after, here with you and our baby. We're a family. I love you. For now and always."

"I love you, too."

As Hayden cuddled beside me and Declan fed in my arms, I imprinted this moment in my mind. I was home. It was time to make new memories. Dream new dreams. Live life to the fullest with no regrets.

Chapter 18

HUNTER

Lying on my bed with my head propped on my hand, I gazed down at my twins. Their little inquisitive dark blue eyes blinked up at me. "I can't believe they're here."

Two boys. Levi and Louis—named after two of Kara's favorite fashion brands—were delivered safely by C-section four days ago on December 1st. Naomi had been incredible as always and was recovering well. But after carrying the twins, she was all babied out. No more surrogacy. We didn't need it. Kara and I had a family.

"They're perfect." Kara stretched out on the other side of our babies. She leaned forward and kissed Louis's forehead.

The only way I could tell the identical twins apart was that Levi had a tiny mole on his lower back in the same place I had one. Louis had one on the back of his right hand.

Ashleigh crawled from playing on the end of the bed to lie beside me and kissed Levi's tummy. "Baba."

"That's right." I swept my hand over Ashleigh's soft brown curls. "That's your baby brother Levi."

Then Ashleigh turned and pulled on the other twin's toes, stretched the onesie like it was an elastic band. "Baba."

"And that's Louis."

We'd brought our two happy, healthy bundles of joy home

from the hospital yesterday. Three and a half weeks before I turned thirty, I had a complete family. Best early birthday present ever.

I leaned over Levi and kissed Kara's gorgeous lips. "You happy, Pearl?"

The smile hadn't left her face since Ashleigh was born. Now, with the addition of twins, her radiance shone brighter than all the stars in the universe.

"More than ever," she whispered. "I have three beautiful babies, an amazing husband, and a gorgeous home." Her eyes glistened with tears. "This is everything I've ever wanted."

As I rubbed Levi's tiny, delicate hand between my fingers, I took in my family—the babies on their backs taking in their new world, Ashleigh growing so fast, and Kara, who grew more and more beautiful every day. "This is more than I ever dreamed of."

From as early as I could remember, I'd dreamed of nothing but music and performing. The astounding heights of success I'd reached had involved many ups and downs, but the good had far outweighed the bad. I'd never contemplated having a family until Kara had gotten pregnant with Ryan. Now, I couldn't imagine anything different.

As Christmas drew closer, life was a haze of feeding babies, diaper changes, and a lack of decent sleep. Two days before Christmas, I dressed my children in warm clothes, placed the twins in one stroller, Ashleigh in another, and grabbed the diaper bag. While the sun shone, we needed to get out of the penthouse and grab some fresh air. I zipped up my anorak and called down the hallway. "You ready, Kar?"

"Coming." She dashed out of our bedroom toward me as I waited by the elevator. She buttoned her long black woolen coat, then wriggled and straightened her beanie and bright blue scarf. With a flick of her hand, she tossed her braid over her shoulder. Her red lipstick turned her lips into alluring treats. The subtle brush of golden eyeshadow above her eyes highlighted the gorgeous deep blue of her irises. Her smile stole my breath.

God, I loved her.

Like I was born to be a rockstar, she'd always wanted to be a mother and a designer. They were her callings in life. While she thanked her therapist for helping her overcome her mental health issues and anxiety, I was convinced it was her reconnecting with fashion design, my love and support, and our children that had restored her happiness.

I caught her hips between my hands, shuffled her back against the wall, and kissed her. Long, slow, and deep. With a little bit of tongue. And a whole lot of *fuck-you're-sexy-and-I-want-you* hunger. I breathed in her floral perfume. Pressing my body against hers ignited the fire in my blood. "You know we're only going to the park? Not a photo shoot."

"Yes. But I've barely left the place for weeks. I wanted to feel human again."

I slid my hand up her side and cupped her breast. "You feel human to me."

"Hmm." She pressed her forehead against mine. "Maybe we should get Diego to babysit this evening. I could do with a date night."

"Are you ready to leave the kids with him already?" Had I heard her correctly?

"A few hours would be okay. It's all about balance, right? Music, fashion, and family. Us time is important too."

"Absolutely." We always had *us* time. When we showered. When we were in bed. Whenever the kids were asleep. But taking Kara out for dinner somewhere nice was well overdue. "I'll call him soon. For now, let's get out of here before my dick won't allow us to leave." It was already protesting. But we needed some fresh air before the fine weather disappeared.

I loaded my family into the elevator and clicked on the stroller brakes. But as we descended, a deep ache loomed in my chest and at the back of my mind. I leaned against the mirrored wall and closed my eyes. I loved my family and loved the time I spent with them. But something was missing. *Music. The fans. Touring.* I'd had a quiet year compared to our previous ones. I'd promised Kara to take time off until after Fashion Week. Two more months seemed like a lifetime.

"Hey?" Kara touched my arm. "Are you okay?"

"Yep. Just tired." I wiped my weary eyes. "Levi kept me awake too long last night." I was used to being up at all hours of the night, so I often did the night feeds. But Levi hadn't settled after his bottle. It had taken me over an hour to get him back to sleep.

After a lazy stroll along the Hudson River, with Mick ambling behind us, we stopped at the kids' playground near one of the piers. While the twins slept in their stroller, I pushed Ashleigh on the baby swing. Her bright blue eyes lit up as she swung through the air. I'd never imagined that simple things like a walk and a play in the park could be so satisfying.

My heart thrummed in time with the squeaks of the swing, up with every one of Ashleigh's smiles, but then . . . down like a booming gong. *Fuck.* I needed to bury my burn for music for a couple more months. I could do that. Dropping a new single after New Year's would pull me through. But with only local radio promo planned, the normal hype, being surrounded by fans, wouldn't be there. My soul craved more fuel.

Kara parked the twins next to me, then leaned her shoulder against the pole of the swing set.

"Hunt?" She tucked her hands into her coat pockets. "You're quiet. You're never quiet."

"I'm just enjoying the sunshine."

"You're such a bad liar." She quirked a smile. "What's up?"

"Um . . ." I stared across the river, my sunglasses dimming the glare shimmering on the surface. I cleared my throat. "Since the twins are good, they're healthy and not too much trouble, I'd like to . . . *shit* . . . no . . . It doesn't matter. I'm cool." I flicked my thoughts away. My family came first.

She tilted her head and rested it against the pole. "You want to start the new album, don't you?"

Damn, she knew me too well. But her tone held no disappointment. I was caught off-guard by the glint in her eyes and the upward curve of her lips.

"Yeah. But it's okay." I swung Ashleigh higher. Her little laughs claimed my heart. "I can wait."

"I'm amazed you lasted this long before the need drove you mad." She glanced down at the twins. "Our babies are the most important thing in the world, but so is our passion. You're the most amazing father, the most supportive husband, but music is who you are. You've been beyond patient waiting for Gem, Kyle, and Hayden to be ready. But I can see the restless fire inside you." She stepped toward me and placed her hand on my chest. Did she feel the beat wanting to be unleashed? "Hunt, we're all about balance now. We've had a crazy few months overloaded with babies. But it's time to reset the scales. If we plan our schedules, throw in a little compromise, and pray we never lose Diego, I say, go for it. Get in that studio. Record. Make the music happen."

I held my breath. "You mean that?"

"Yeah. I do."

"Arggggh." I clutched her face and kissed her. "You're the best. I love you so freaking much. Thank you."

My God. My mind spun. My heart drummed to a wicked new beat.

The sooner my band recorded, the sooner we could release the album, start promo, and plan the tour. I couldn't wait to roll out new music and hit the stage. Fuck, I loved performing, singing, and entertaining a crowd. And this time when we traveled, my family would be by my side. Life couldn't get much better than that.

I couldn't wait to tell my friends. They were as desperate as I was to make new music. I'd break the news to them at Christmas. It was only two days away.

Could I contain the news for that long? I hoped so. As long as Gemma and her freaky intuition didn't come into play.

This would be the best Christmas present for everyone.

The need to hit the studio called to us.

It was time to make new music.

We'd waited long enough.

Chapter 19

GEMMA

A sea of Christmas gift bags, boxes, and wrapping paper littered Hunter's living room floor and the coffee table. Laughter and chatter filled the air. I let my head sink back against the sofa's headrest. The love that cascaded from my heart had nothing to do with the magnificent Christmas tree covered in twinkling lights standing by the window, or the carols playing softly through the sound system, or the delicious smell of dinner roasting in the kitchen, or the overwhelming generosity of gifts. It had everything to do with my family—Kyle, my friends, and our children.

Beside me, Skye slept on Kyle's shoulder. She was curled into a ball and wrapped in a fluffy white blanket. Her long eyelashes brushed her chubby cheeks. With her tiny lips and petite nose, she was undoubtedly as cute as a baby bunny. To my right, Hunter sat next to me, then Kara. They each held one twin, feeding them a bottle. Ashleigh's head lay on Kara's lap; she was sound asleep after a huge Christmas day with Kara's family. Adjacent to Kyle, Hayden snuggled next to Lexi as Declan fed. It was a true Polaroid moment.

But as I drew in a deep breath and glanced at my friends, something else hovered in the air. Something that was more magical than spending Christmas night with loved ones. It was a force that couldn't be reckoned with. It was like the day I'd met Hunter and Kyle, only it was even more powerful than that. It was as if destiny had been fulfilled. An unbreakable bond had been forged. Happiness and contentment had been achieved.

These people had unquestionably renewed my faith in love, rewired my notion of family, and had re-tuned my want to be a mother.

Was it wrong to feel so blessed? Would this state of happiness last? Who knew? But I would treasure every moment that it did.

It would be even more relaxing if Hunter stopped wriggling and jiggling and straightening his legs. Stopped crossing them, then drawing them in and swaying his knees from side to side.

I slapped him on the thigh. "Sit still."

Something was bothering him. I had yet to get to the bottom of it. I'd do that after we finished exchanging gifts. Poor Levi would be sick with Hunter's shuffling around.

I curled into Kyle's side, draped my arm across his waist, and kissed him on the cheek. "You want me to take Skye?"

It was our turn for gifts, and Kyle had our present for everyone.

I rubbed Skye's tiny booty-covered foot; she didn't even flinch. "She looks very content with you, though." After I'd had a rough pregnancy, Skye had been a dream baby. She rarely woke during the night. Didn't vomit. And rarely cried. *Thank goodness.*

"She loves her daddy." Kyle rested his cheek against Skye's petite head.

"You spoil her."

"Hell yeah."

Hunter jutted his chin toward the plush ponies, musical play sets, and bags of building blocks lying on the floor. "By the quantity of baby crap here, I'd say we all spoiled our kids." His legs jiggled again.

"We certainly did." I picked up the plush green dinosaur I'd bought the twins, then smacked Hunter in the arm with it. I'd had enough of his jostling around. "Hunt, what's up?"

"Nothing. Just love you."

Liar.

He tapped my thigh, then leaned the other way toward Kara and kissed her on the lips. "But I love you even more."

Kara blushed and rested her cheek against his shoulder. Pure joy lit her face as she cradled Louis, gazed at Levi, and stroked Ashleigh's bouncing curls. The happiness radiating from her struck me right in the center of my chest.

I peered around Hunter at Kara. "I'm so stoked you have the family you've always wanted."

"It's still surreal." Tears welled in Kara's eyes. "All my dreams have come true."

Lexi finished feeding Declan and handed him to Hayden. "I can't believe we all have children."

Hayden sat Declan on his thigh, cupped his tiny milk-drunk face in one hand, and rubbed and patted his back with the other. Declan's little eyes were closed, and drool dribbled from the corner of his mouth. "It's awesome that we've had families at the same time. Our kids will grow up together. That's so cool."

"Talking about growing up together . . ." Kyle carefully handed Skye to me to hold.

I cradled her in my arms and kissed her forehead.

Skye, my mini-Kyle, was the best mistake I'd ever made. She was perfect. She'd brought Kyle and me closer together. I honestly hadn't thought that was possible. But creating life had done so.

"It's time for another present." Kyle leaned sideways and pulled a large, folded envelope out of the back pocket of his jeans. My heart rate doubled, knowing what it contained. He tapped the envelope against his palm. "You guys mean the world to Gem and me. We never tire of living out of each other's pockets, making music, touring, and sharing our homes with you. And we don't ever want that to change. So, our Christmas present to everyone is this." He pulled out a piece of paper from the envelope, unfolded it, and smoothed it out on the coffee table. "I've talked to an architect, and this is a preliminary design for renovating and extending our beach house at Amagansett so we can all fit."

"Holy shit." Hunter leaned forward over Levi, put the empty baby bottle down, and grabbed the piece of paper. "What the hell?" He scanned the new floorplans. "You wanna turn your great grandparents' rundown shack into this? A one. Two. Three . . . shit . . . an eight bedroom home. With a studio. A new kitchen. A media room. *Fuck.* You sure about this, bud?"

"Yes." Kyle twisted his new leather cuff from me around his wrist. "It's time to turn the worst house on the road to being on par with the rest of the neighborhood. The renovations will turn this place into a destination where we can spend vacations together. Y'all can use it at any time, with or without us."

I curled my hand around Kyle's thigh. The beach house held a ton of memories within its walls—my first kiss with Kyle on the deck, the first time we'd slept together, the parties, summer vacations, and quick getaways. But just like we had, the house needed to evolve.

I tilted my head toward Kara. "Are you fine with this?"

Kara had struggled with staying there in the past. She'd been there after losing Ryan, and that memory had haunted her.

Kara's gaze softened and she nodded. "Yeah. I am. I have a family now. Spending vacations there will fill my head and heart with new memories. Playing with the kids on the beach, swimming, and building sandcastles will be perfect."

"Kyle? Gem?" Hayden rubbed his hand over his face. "You don't have to renovate to accommodate us. You've done so much for Lex and me already. We are forever in your debt."

"No, you're not." I shook my head. "You're one of us."

"This is incredible. Thank you." Lexi curled her feet beneath her. "Vacations together have always been fun. I look forward to many more. But even more than that, I can't wait until the next tour. I want to travel and see more of the world and take photos in every city we visit. It will be interesting with five kids between us. We're gonna need to hire a semi just for the baby gear."

Tour? My heart jolted and jerked. My Christmas glow plowed headfirst into the snow. Our next tour seemed so distant. The embers simmered inside my soul, ready to ignite. I couldn't wait to work on our new album. I itched to get back into the studio. March seemed so far away. "We'll do whatever it takes. I just want to tour again."

As Hunter lifted Levi onto his shoulder, he nudged his knee against my leg. His eyes blazed bright. "Gem? Just how bad do you want to tour? How bad do you want to start the album?"

Cheekiness skipped through my veins as I held Skye toward him. "I'd give you my firstborn baby."

"Ah . . . no thanks." Hunter chuckled and held up his hand. "I have enough kids of my own."

Thank goodness. I smiled as I pressed a soft kiss against Skye's cheek. My daughter smelled of milk and baby powder and freshly laundered clothes. *Perfect.* I wouldn't give her up for the world—not even music.

"Well, then." A huge smile crept across Hunter's face. "My Christmas present to you, in addition to the journals I gave you, is a new date. Let's move the start date of the album forward. To now. To the new year. To whatever day suits everyone."

"What?" I straightened. My pulse flickered faster than the Christmas lights on the tree. "To now. Now suits me. Like right now."

"Oh my God, yes." Kyle shot forward to the edge of the sofa. "I've been ready for months."

"Me too." Hayden raised Declan into the air. "Woohoo. It's music time." But Declan didn't seem to care, already half asleep after his feed. Hayden chuckled, placed Declan over his shoulder and patted his baby's bum. *Too sweet.*

Hunter grinned. "I love my family, but fuck, I need music too."

"We all do." Excitement skipped in my voice. "I have all these songs and lyrics and tunes in my head. I don't know how we'll manage, but we'll work around the kids, and sleep, and schedules. I just need to get back in the studio with you guys and make music."

Lexi jutted her chin at Kara. "But what about Fashion Week? I thought you wanted them to record after the next showing?"

As Kara cradled Louis in her arms, she rounded her shoulders and smiled at everyone. "These guys have delayed hitting the studio for long enough. After New Year's, I'll be at Ivory's two or three days a week; they can work here in the home studio. Diego can mind the kids at either your place or Kyle and Gem's. Then, in mid-February, after Fashion Week, we can all head up to Woodstock as planned."

The guys and I had rebooked the mansion upstate where we'd written our last album. Reynold, our production engineer, and a couple of sound technicians would join us once we'd created some tracks. We'd write, record, and produce the album in its entirety while we were there.

Fire flickered in Hunter's eyes. "If we do shorter days while here and be home every night for the kids, this will work. We don't want Diego to burn out."

My engines roared to life. I could sense the steel strings of my guitar beneath my fingers, hear the tunes playing in my head, and feel the drumbeats in my heart. Starting the album now meant we'd hit promo earlier, release the album sooner, and get back on the road ahead of schedule. *Yes. Yes. YES!*

"I'll be around to help too," Lexi added. "You're only a block away if I need Hayden to come home or if Diego needs a hand. I can drop in here to grab footage and photos of you at work. I'll do the same for you, Kara, when you're at Ivory's. This will be awesome."

I squealed and wriggled on the sofa, careful not to wake Skye. *This* was what Hunter had been keeping from me. "Oh, wow! An earlier date is brilliant. I want to start now."

Kyle chuckled, hooked his arm behind me, and rubbed the back of my head. "How about we wait until after Christmas?"

I might be crazy returning to work. Skye was only three months old. But like the guys, music burned in my veins. It was a fire that couldn't be contained.

Every day with Skye was a learning curve, a very steep, windy, and sometimes bumpy road. But being a mom didn't mean I had to change who I was. I was a musician, a performer and now . . . a mother. Kyle was a phenomenal father. He fed Skye at night, changed her, and played with her. The love I had for him and our daughter was endless. The love I had for my friends and their children, boundless. My love for music, limitless.

Kyle caught my chin, turned it toward him, and kissed my lips. "Are you sure you're ready to do this? Ready to make music?"

Couldn't he hear how loud my heart was beating? "Always."

I gazed at Skye sleeping in my arms, at Levi curled against Hunter's chest, at Louis and Ashleigh snoozing on Kara, and at Declan, out like a light on Hayden's shoulder. So much love flowed across this room that it overwhelmed me.

This family and music were everything.

Leaning against Kyle, with Skye in my embrace, the song the guys and I had written for our partners and babies tumbled softly from my lips.

The moment I met you, something changed in me
The way I felt defied all gravity
Every time I look at you, my heart just races
I tried to fight it as you put me through my paces

Kyle joined in, singing in perfect harmony.

The moment I heard your voice, the angels guided me
Can't deny we were oh so meant to be
Every time I look at you, my soul sets on fire
I tried to fight it, but you make me so high, yeah

You claimed my heart, captured my soul
Now you're mine, I can never ever let go

Just so you know . . .
I'll watch over you when you are sleeping
Clear the clouds when you are dreaming
Let you catch all the stars in the night sky
Love you every day that goes by and by

Hunter kissed Kara on the cheek, then joined in the chorus, singing in his low, husky voice.

> *The moment I saw you, I knew fate had a plan for us*
> *But who knew where the universe would take us?*
> *Every day is like a new beginning*
> *My love for you will be never ending*
> *I tried to fight it, but you're my reason for living*

Hayden seamlessly joined in. His alto voice added a perfect, rich tone to our sound.

> *You claimed my heart, captured my soul*
> *Now you're mine, I can never ever let go*
>
> *Just so you know . . .*
> *I'll watch over you when you're sleeping*
> *Clear the clouds when you're dreaming*
> *Let you catch all the stars in the night sky*
> *Love you every day that goes by and by*

I nudged my elbow against Hunter's arm, then twisted my head toward Kyle. My eyes pricked with tears.

What a journey I'd been on with these two men. My best friends. My lover and my brother from another mother.

And our story wasn't over yet.

The people who had come in and out of our lives had made our connection stronger and our lives better. We had grown from being three lone teenagers into an unmistakable united front. Kara, Lexi, and Hayden completed our tight-knit circle. Our forged ring was unbreakable, bound by love. We'd become an incredible family of eleven. With each other's unquestionable love and undying support, our future would only get bigger, brighter and better. One thing was certain: nothing would ever tear my Everhide family apart. We would be together . . . forever.

Epilogue

GEMMA

On December twenty-seventh, the day after Hunter's thirtieth birthday, I lugged my acoustic and electric guitars into Hunter's studio and propped the cases near the rack. I dumped my laptop bag, stuffed full of notebooks and my computer, on the coffee table. That bag held scribbled thoughts, jotted down lyrics, and random riffs I'd worked on over many years. I'd combine them with the material from the guys, then we'd sifted through our ideas, messed around with melodies, and turned moments into magic.

Kyle stood his bass against the piano and came over to stand in front of me. He swept my hair back behind my shoulders. "You all set?"

"Absolutely."

Skye and the kids were at our place. Diego seemed to be in his element looking after them. I was more than ready to get to work.

Hayden flopped on the sofa, drumsticks in hand. Nerves flitted through his gaze. But he had nothing to worry about. After working with him on the singles we'd written, he fitted seamlessly into our creative process.

Hunter came into the studio carrying a tray loaded with hot coffees—the perfect way to start the day. He handed everyone a cup. "Get this into you."

After taking a sip, I grabbed my acoustic guitar and pulled up a stool by the coffee table. My heart struck a steady beat against my ribs. "Let's make music, guys."

Hayden downed a mouthful of his coffee, then shuffled through some pages of lyrics, glared at Kyle's open laptop with recording software on the screen, and then at Hunter's journal. "So . . . how do you guys start an album? Do you create a mood board? Come up with a story? A sound? A theme?"

Hunter chuckled. "Fuck no. That happened when we were with SureHaven, but now, we just write from the heart. That morphs into a life of its own. We write what we're feeling, what we've experienced, what we're going through, what we dream about. Basically, it comes from where we are at in life."

Hayden rubbed the back of his neck. "So, you get all touchy-feely."

"Yep." I took a sip of my drink. The caffeine zipped through my veins. Just the kick-starter I needed. "But you could have guessed that."

This was the first full-length album Hayden had ever been involved in. When he was with his former band, their lead singer, Kilt, had written all the songs. But Hayden had incredible talent. We'd heard some of the songs he'd written, and they were phenomenal. We planned to nurture his skills, make him even better and bring out the best in him. I knew we would.

I strummed and tuned a string. "This room will prove to be better than therapy. We'll dig deep into our feelings, our fears, our desires. We'll laugh. We'll cry. We'll support and trust each other. We'll never judge. No idea will go left unheard. No tune or beat or riff will remain un-played."

"Gem has a cool way of drawing out our first song." Kyle wheeled his stool closer to the coffee table. "She's a genius with lyrics."

"What?" I jerked my chin back. "Just lyrics? I'm way more than that, baby."

"That you are." He leaned forward over his bass and gave me a quick kiss on the lips.

Hunter finished his coffee and picked up his rhythm guitar from beside the sofa. He hooked the strap over his head and swiveled on the office chair beside me. "Let's do this."

"Okay." Hayden shuffled to the edge of the sofa and rolled his drumsticks against his thigh. "What do we do?"

I smiled at him. So did the guys.

"Tell us how you're feeling?" I asked.

Hayden stilled his sticks. "Nervous."

Yep, his hands shook.

"Close your eyes for me. What was one moment in your life that made you break out in a sweat, sick to the stomach, and had you question your sanity?"

"That's easy," Hayden smirked. "On top of the countless times I've shat my pants playing for you, I'll never forget the night at Wembley Stadium. That was sick."

"What made it different from any other night?" I kept with my line of questioning.

"The size of the place. The deafening sound. The screaming. The sea of fans. I didn't want to fuck up playing. I was so terrified, but so . . ."

I remembered my first night at Wembley years ago. It had been gob-smacking. We'd played at the stadium a couple of times now. It still blew my mind that ninety thousand people filled the venue. That they'd come to see us perform. The moment the fans had hollered our name, I'd wanted to give them the best show ever. Give them my all. "So . . . what, Hayds?"

Hayden rubbed his chest. His brow furrowed. His closed eyes tightened further. Yeah . . . I had him right where I wanted him. He sucked in a deep breath. "So overwhelmed. I was where I belonged. I was where I was meant to be. I was doing what I loved with the people I love, and I want to do that for the rest of my life. I was there, living my dream, because of you guys."

So many people never fulfilled their dreams, but the guys and

I had achieved every one of ours. Finding each other had filled our lives with loyal friendships, fun times, uncanny love, bold truth, and undeniable fate. Time had brought us even closer together. We'd become a family. There was no turning back.

"Destiny brought us together." I threw Hayden a heartfelt smile as I tapped my pen against my notebook. Lyrics swirled through my head and came alive. I mumbled some words, jotted them down, then reworked a few lines. I tapped my foot to match the beat in my brain and sang in a low, slow, and sultry voice.

> *It was like lightning*
> *That struck with no warning*
> *It was like sunshine*
> *After days of rain*
> *I was always searching*
> *Looking for something*
> *Didn't know what it was until I found you*
> *Until I found you*
>
> *It took a single heartbeat*
> *A moment to draw in air*
> *Something happened to me*
> *Right then and right there*

I filled my lungs to capacity, then sang faster, doubling the tempo.

> *Chills ran up my spine, curled through my veins and claimed my heart*
> *Don't care what everyone says, I know we'll never part*
> *They say we'll never make it; I had to prove them wrong*
> *Standing here, holding your hand, is where . . . where I belong*

"Fuck, Gem." Hayden stared at my page of words. "You just came up with that out of nothing."

"It's not nothing. It's a memory. It's a feeling. It's understanding that some nights can be overwhelming. It's about *us*. Finding each other and doing what we love."

"You are freakishly talented." His eyes glinted as he shook his head and rubbed the back of his head.

"I just love expressing moments through music." I wriggled in my chair and pointed my pen at Hunter. "What about you? What is something that spins your mind about life lately?"

He puffed air through his nose and touched his throat. "After my vocal cord dramas, I'm stoked I have a voice to sing with." Then, he placed his hand over his heart. "And I'm blown away that I have Kar and the kids." He rested his arm on top of his guitar. "I'll never take my voice for granted. But, man . . . The kids? They're nothing short of a miracle. After everything Kar and I have been through—the loss, the heartache, and pain—finally having them is amazing. It chokes me up every time I look at them. I'm so fucking lucky to have my family. They're everything, Gem."

I wanted to wrap my arms around him and hug him tight. He'd become a doting dad and smitten husband. *So cool.* He'd changed, but then . . . I had, too.

Digging deep, I drew on Hunter's past and his present. Lyrics spilled onto my page. As I hummed and sang, Hunter played around with some chords, catching onto my tune. Kyle strummed his bass. Hayden joined in, tapping his sticks on the coffee table.

> *It was like daylight*
> *After the darkest night*
> *My heart was nothing*
> *Until I saw you*
> *I was always searching*
> *Looking for something*
> *Didn't know what it was until I found you*
> *Until I found you*
>
> *It took a single heartbeat,*
> *A moment to draw in air*
> *Something happened to me,*

Right then and right there

Chills ran up my spine, curled through my veins and claimed my heart
Don't care what everyone says, I know we'll never part
They say we'll never make it; I had to prove them wrong
Standing here, holding your hand, is where . . . where I belong

I re-read the lyrics. Songs always held magic when they incorporated something about each of us, our experiences, and emotions. It gave the words more meaning, and we'd put more heart and soul into singing them.

I flicked my hair back and turned to Kyle. "Babe, what about you?"

"What overwhelms me?" His gaze softened as he leaned closer. He lowered his voice. "What blows my mind? What am I in awe of every day?"

I shrugged. "Yeah. Something along those lines."

"You."

My heart fluttered like a butterfly, dipping and darting through the sky. The love in his espresso eyes stole my breath.

"Gem, none of this life would have happened if it wasn't for you." He stroked my hair, then tucked the loose strands behind my ear. "From that day back in high school when you begged me to teach you to play piano better, to asking to play with Hunt and me, to the contests we entered, to the record deals we signed, to the songs we've written, the tours we've done, and now, the family we have. It's all thanks to you."

He claimed my heart all over again. "You're so sweet. I love you." I touched his cheek and kissed him.

"Okay, you two. Enough." Hunter laughed as he clipped the back of my head with his hand. "It's day one, for fuck's sake. Gem, write the damn song."

Hayden waved his drumsticks at Kyle and me. "Are you always like this?"

"Wait until we write a love song." I threw him a saucy smile, spun my pen around in my fingertips, then turned to my page. He hadn't seen anything yet. I couldn't help it if Kyle turned me on . . . a lot. And we had to take breaks from writing.

I closed my eyes. Visions of Kyle filled my head. His gorgeous smile, his gorgeous eyes, and his golden tan. His body toned to perfection. But our connection was beyond physical attraction; our souls had entwined on the day we'd met. Sixteen years on, our love only grew stronger and stronger.

I held my pen over the page and wrote what was in my heart. The bridge and chorus for the song were cemented in my mind. I licked my lips and sang low and breathy again.

> *It took a single heartbeat*
> *A moment to draw in air*
> *Something happened to me*
> *Right then and right there*
>
> *It took me by surprise, but I think I've found my forever*
> *You stole my breath, stole my heart, bound our souls together*
>
> *I want to spend all my hours breathing the very same air as you*
> *I want to spend all my days discovering what it's like to be loved by you*
> *I want to spend all my years living life and growing old right next to you*
> *I count all my blessings every day and night since I found you*
> *Since I found you*

I glanced from Kyle to Hayden to Hunter. I'd certainly found my forever.

Right here. With these guys. Making music.

We played around with the tune. It morphed. It changed. It evolved into a track.

One track led to the next. And the next. And the next.

Day after day, songs poured out of us. Beats and rhythms and tunes took form.

By the time we'd headed to Woodstock in mid-February, we had several songs completed. We'd balanced long days writing and recording with time with our new family lives. Kids, music, and hanging out with friends were our new norm.

After six weeks upstate, the album was cut. Singles were selected. Promo had been scheduled. A new tour was planned.

Following a month of endless meetings, fittings at fashion houses, dressing for photo shoots, video clip filming, and partaking in interviews, I stood with the guys and stared up at the brightest, biggest billboard in Times Square. The cover image of our first single, "I Found You"—our ode to Hayden joining us and the very first song we'd penned for our new album—*Bound By Love*—filled the screen. The four of us lazed about on a red velvet loveseat in the center of a forest.

A new era of Everhide was born.

The cool late April breeze brushed my cheek. I draped my arm around Kyle's back and hooked my finger through the belt loop on his jeans. Life was about to catapult us into the fast lane again. The promo for our new single, jet-setting across the globe, and visiting four countries, started tomorrow.

Life had changed. Kyle and I juggled work and Skye. Everyone else did the same with their families. Diego traveled everywhere with us and our kids. At every break, after every show or at the end of every day, Kyle and I rushed home to be with our daughter, to give her cuddles and kisses, read her stories, play with her, or put her to bed. I wouldn't have it any other way. I had music and a family. I was determined to make being a mom and a rockstar work, and I'd ride this rush with my friends to the end of my days. Until I drew my very last breath.

***

Five packed suitcases stood in a line by the front door. Guitars were stacked beside them, stowed away in their cases. So was a baby stroller, a portable crib, and a Gucci trunk loaded with baby gear. With Skye propped on my hip, I glanced around my home one last time. In my heart, I was ready to rush out the door, but I wanted to stay put as well. We'd be gone, traveling around the world for the next eleven months. Had I packed everything we needed for Skye? Had I forgotten anything *I* needed for the tour?

Kyle wove his arms around my waist and caressed our daughter's head. He dipped his chin and kissed my lips. "Are you ready to do it all again?"

The album was out. Singles had been released. Promo had been completed. It was time for our sixth world tour.

I'd trained, rehearsed, and knew our set list backward. "You bet."

Skye wriggled in my arms and reached for Kyle. He lifted her from my grasp, held her against his chest and kissed her chubby cheek. "You ready too, sweet pea?"

Skye had just turned thirteen months old. She looked more and more like Kyle every day with her soft, silky dark blond hair, big brown eyes that stole my heart, and olive skin just like his. And boy, was she a handful. She'd walked at ten months old. Kyle and I struggled to keep up with her. She was a bundle of energy and bright as a spark. And my heart exploded every time she laughed and smiled. I'd never thought a baby, *my* baby, would've had that effect on me. The smile that lit Kyle's face every time he was with Skye was just magical. He loved her so much. He loved me just the same. *This* was family.

Our door buzzed. Kyle let in Sam and Chester, our security team, and Marcus, our doorman, to grab our luggage.

"Ready to hit the road?" Sam tucked a guitar case under each burly arm and grabbed a suitcase in each hand.

"We sure are." I nodded and grabbed a bag.

"I thought you guys had a lot of shit last tour." Chester gathered as much luggage as he could carry. "But now, with kids? This is insane."

"This is nothing." Kyle smirked. "Wait until you see what Kara has packed."

"Shit." Chester sighed. "I have two suitcases, folks. Two. For a year of travel, that's it."

"I remember those days." I giggled and sighed.

Years ago, when we'd just started out, Kyle and I had traveled with just about every item of clothing we'd owned in one or two cases. Now, we had bags and trunks of outfits for our shows, events, and everyday living. Thankfully, most of our gear had been shipped with our staging equipment.

I hooked the diaper bag and my purse over my shoulder, then grabbed Skye's backpack off the floor. "Let's go. Only one hundred and seventeen shows until we're home."

"Are we crazy for doing this?" Kyle's eyes glinted as he brushed his fingertips over my chin. He was as itchy as I was to get onstage in front of the crowds.

"Possibly." I stood on my tippy-toes and kissed his lips. "But we're gonna own it. Rock it. And kick butt every night." I smacked him on his hot ass . . . twice. "Let's go."

We loaded our gear onto the bus, picked up our friends, and headed to the private airport, bound for Italy. Opening night of our *Bound by Love* tour would be in front of eighty thousand fans at the San Siro Stadium in Milan.

At the airport, electric energy hovered around my friends and entourage as we gathered in the VIP lounge. Bec hugged me hello, then tickled Skye's socked feet. "Hey, monkey. You ready to go on a plane? Don't you cause any trouble for Auntie Bec, okay? Your mom will do enough of that."

Skye giggled and buried her head into my neck.

"You all set?" I asked Bec.

"Absolutely." Bec nodded. "Everyone's here. We're ready to go."

Kate and Sophie stood with their partners, who'd be joining them for the first leg of the tour. Olsen, our tour manager, Floyd, our head sound engineer, Clinton, and Carla lingered by the bar. The other ninety-seven crew members of our tour group would travel on a different plane to us. They were already on their way to Milan.

From the caterers, to the road crew, to the equipment technicians, the sound engineers, and our entourage, we were all one big Everhide family—ready to take on the world.

"Let's go then." I nodded.

On the private plane, my heart raced as I settled into my soft leather seat with Skye on my lap. Kyle buckled in beside me. Hunter and Kara were across the aisle, holding the twins. Lexi and Hayden were in front of them with Declan. Diego sat nearby with Ashleigh. The long days ahead, our grueling schedule, and the physical toll the tour took on my body worried me. But my amazing team, the godsend of Diego and my friends, would help me through everything. Skye would be with Kyle and me, every step of the way. Whenever we finished an interview, hung out backstage after a sound check, returned to the hotel after a show, or traveled many miles, she'd always be with us. Our daughter would never feel unwanted or unloved. She'd never be abandoned.

As the plane rumbled down the runway and lifted into the air, tears welled in my eyes. It felt like a lifetime ago since Kyle, Hunter and I had boarded a plane to LA after we'd won the "Discovered on YouTube" contest. Back to the time when our heads were filled with dreams and aspirations of becoming a world-famous rock band. When Kyle and I had penned one of our first hits: "Horizon."

Don't care if we fly
Don't care if we run
Don't care how we're gonna get there
Just gonna follow the sun

So, take my hand
We'll soar above the clouds
Follow our dreams
Never gonna touch the ground

Yee-yeah-ya. Yee-yeah-ya, Yee-yeah, yeah

We'll aim for the horizon
Don't know when we'll be home again
So baby, come on, come with me
Don't know where this road will end

Let's aim for the horizon
Let's touch the stars
Sail across the oceans
Follow our beating hearts

With you by my side
We're gonna touch the sky
Gonna love you forever
'Til the day I die
'Til the day I die

We'd surpassed the horizon. We'd achieved all our dreams and more. We'd found love, happiness, and had families. I'd love them until the day I died.

As I sucked in a deep breath, my heart filled my chest. I gave Skye a big cuddle and kissed the top of her head, and gazed into Kyle's beautiful eyes. I had everything I'd ever wanted and more than I had ever imagined.

I had Kyle, my love, my soul mate.

I had Skye, my gorgeous daughter.

I had incredible friends.

I had music and my Everhide family.

Kyle leaned toward me and kissed my lips. His citrusy cologne filled my senses. "I love you." His smile held me captive. "Every time we go on tour, I never forget where we started—that first trip to LA." *Was he reading my mind? Again?* "We've reached the stars, sailed across many oceans, and we're doing what we love every day. So, what's next for us, Gem? What do we do now that we're at the top of our game and have everything we've ever wanted?"

I caressed his smooth cheek. "Can we just be happy? Love our daughter and our friends? And make music for the rest of our days?"

"I like the sound of that."

"Me too," I whispered against his lips. "I love you. Always and forever. But for now, let's go rock the world."

"I'm in." He pressed his soft, tender lips against mine. He smiled then deepened our kiss. The gentle flicks of his tongue were warm, sensual, and seductive. *Pure heaven.* My love for him charged through my veins and found a home in my heart. He would always be my rock, my grounding, my four-four common time—just what I'd always needed.

***

Taking the stage on the first night of the tour, with the crowd screaming, waving their banners, and clicking their cell phone cameras, I slayed my guitar. Kyle and Hunter jammed beside me. Behind us, Hayden held the set together, smashing out our hits on the drums. I stepped up to the mic, pumped my fist in the air, and hollered, "*Ciao Milano. Siete pronti per il rock?*"

"Yeah!" The audience clapped and shrieked.

Cool. My Italian didn't suck.

I laughed and let the music fill my soul. Pumping out our songs, playing it up to the crowd, and putting on a show fueled the fire in my heart, but now, so did something else. Something more rewarding, more mind-blowing, more precious and powerful.

My family.

From this point on, every chord, every concert, every churned-out hit would now and always be for Kyle, for Skye . . . and my Everhide family. They were, and always would be, my reason for living.

Music was life. Family was everything.

. . . And Everhide would rock on forever.

***

Thank you for reading my Everhide Rockstar Romance Series. I hope you loved Kyle and Gemma, Hunter and Kara, and Lexi and Hayden as much as I do.

But wait . . . there's more.

I have a new rockstar series AND a FREE book for you.

With cameos from Everhide, my off-shoot series, **The Flintlocks**, is bound to steal your heart.

Be prepared to fall in love with Flint, Lewis, Cole and Slip.

Start this new series today with Book 1: SCARRED STRINGS - a fake dating rockstar romance.

AVAILABLE ON AMAZON and KINDLE UNLIMITED

P.S. If you enjoyed **RETUNED – The Price of Time**, would you kindly take a moment and leave a quick product review. They are music for an author's soul.

Thank you,
Tania Joyce

BEFORE YOU GO.

Would you like a BONUS EBOOK for FREE?

Find out how my world of rockstars began with the Everhide Rockstar Romance series.

ROCKED – The Price of Dreams is the origin story to my bestselling Everhide Series. Find out how the band met in high school, experience their heartbreak and hardships, and follow their journey to stardom. It is the pre-romance to the adult relationships that develop, evolve, and change throughout the six books. (Three standalones, three follow-ons—all happily ever afters, no cliffhangers).

This series will have you falling in love, shedding tears, and laughing out loud.

Read the prequel, **ROCKED – The Price of DREAMS,** for **FREE** when you subscribe to my newsletter. I only send emails about once a month, so your inbox won't be inundated with my news. Please subscribe here: https://taniajoyce.com/subscribe.

OTHER BOOKS BY TANIA JOYCE

Rockstars, bad boys and billionaires . . . something for everyone.
For eBooks visit Amazon. Paperbacks are available at all
good online book retailers. Author Signed Copies and Bookplates
are available from my website.

The Flintlocks Series

The Everhide Series

Billionaires and College Romance

NEWSLETTER

For information about my new releases, events, and special offers, please subscribe to my monthly newsletter.
Join at: https://taniajoyce.com/subscribe
REMEMBER: You get a BONUS BOOK if you join.

***

FOLLOW TANIA JOYCE

You can follow and find Tania Joyce on the following social media platforms.

Amazon: https://amazon.com/author/taniajoyce
BookBub: https://www.bookbub.com/authors/tania-joyce
Facebook: https://www.facebook.com/taniajoycebooks
Goodreads: https://www.goodreads.com/taniajoyce
Instagram: https://www.instagram.com/taniajoycebooks/
Pinterest: https://www.pinterest.com/taniajoycebooks
TikTok: https://www.tiktok.com/@taniajoyce
Web: http://taniajoyce.com

ABOUT TANIA JOYCE

Tania Joyce is an author of rockstar, contemporary and new adult romance novels. Her stories thread romance, drama and passion into beautiful locations ranging from the dazzling lights and glitter of New York to the rural countryside of the Hunter Valley.

She's widely traveled, has a diverse background in the corporate world and has a love for sparkles, shoes and shiraz.

Tania draws on her real-life experiences and combines them with her very vivid imagination to form the foundation of her novels. She likes to write about strong-minded, career-oriented heroes and heroines that go through drama-filled hell, have steamy encounters and risk everything as they endeavor to find their happy-ever-after.

Tania shuffles the hours in her day between part-time work, family life and writing. One day she hopes to find balance!

She loves to hear from her readers.

Visit: www.taniajoyce.com
or email her at: tania@taniajoyce.com

***

MORE BY TANIA JOYCE

Visit Tania Joyce on Amazon.Com

www.ingramcontent.com/pod-product-compliance
Lightning Source LLC
Chambersburg PA
CBHW060553190726
48283CB00003B/994